Have you signed up for my newsletter yet?

I send out exclusive sneak peeks of all my new releases and giveaways plus a periodic newsletter where we can get to know each other. I'd love to have you. And, as a special thank you for being a part of my News Friends, I will send you a link to download a FREE eBook copy of my novella, *Of Walls*. You can sign up here:

http://eepurl.com/cfqP5H

Would you like a FREE book? For being part of my News Friends, you can receive a free ebook copy of my women's fiction novella, Of Walls.

Also by Sara L. Foust

THE BLUDGEONING OF KIRK JOHNSON

Smoky Mountain Suspense Book Four

Sara L. Foust

The Bludgeoning of Kirk Johnson, Smoky Mountain Suspense Book Four

©2023 Sara L. Foust

Published by Silver Lining Literary Services, LLC
219 Fox Jones Rd
Lancing, TN 37770
www.saralfoust.com

Printed in the United States of America

ISBN: 978-1-7329047-8-1

Scripture quoted is from the King James Version of the Bible, which is in public domain.

For Korrie

My scrappy, smart, sweet fourth baby. You are so strong, and that strength will take you so far. I love you, little munchkin.

And we know that all things work together for good to them that love God, to them who are called according to *his* purpose.

Romans 8:28 KJV

Chapter One

Annalise had never entered the medical examiner's office and felt trapped in a cold dungeon. In fact, Dr. Howard had decorated the room in such a quaint way as to feel homey. With paintings of oceans, prairies, and mountains decorating the light blue walls and windows facing the trees outside, it elicited a sense of peace.

Until today.

Special Agent Annalise Baker waited outside the door with her hands fisted in tight, white-knuckled knots and her heart hammering in her chest. She swallowed back fierce nausea and had to command her lungs to keep breathing. In. Out. In…

Until someone she loved waited on the other side of that door.

"Ready?" Her partner/best friend/boyfriend, Special Agent Zach Leebow, waited at her left elbow.

She shook her head.

He placed a firm hand on her lower back. "Me neither."

"How are we supposed to—" She choked on the next words and quickly brushed a streak of tears from each cheek.

"I don't know," Zach whispered as he gathered her in his embrace.

"I can't…"

"We have to. For him." He released her, kissed the top of her head, and opened the door for her to enter first.

Annalise paused. Drew a deep breath and held it in her chest. She can't… can't see him like that again. What's left of Kirk was… wasn't Kirk.

Chapter Two

Five days earlier…

"Good, Zach. Good." Annalise smiled.

"I'm not a child, Lise."

Boy, did she know that. One look at his muscled chest and the biceps that rippled under his brown uniform and she needed a deep breath. She swallowed and refocused on his exercises. "But you're doing so good."

He rolled his eyes. "Oh yeah?" Instead of touching his left finger to his nose, as he had been repetitively doing for the last five minutes of at-home—at-work?—occupational therapy, he tweaked hers.

"Hey. Not your prescribed therapy, mister." She giggled and scooted her rolling chair farther from him.

Sunlight streamed through her office window, giving the illusion of warmth to their twenty-degree November afternoon. The sun may not provide much heat, but Zach's close proximity burned her from the inside out. She scooched a little farther back and bumped into her desk.

He grinned that toothy smile she'd known and loved for more than three decades. "You okay there?"

Her cheeks flushed. "I'm fine. Break time over."

"Lise, I'm doing so much better. And we don't have a case right now. Let's get lunch."

"Of course, you'd bring up food. It's only eleven."

"Perfect."

"Would you have said that at any time?"

"Do you really have to ask?" His right eyebrow shot upward.

"Nope. I know you."

He stared at her long enough to make her squirm. "You know me. You certainly do, Lise."

Kirk stuck his head in her open office door, interrupting the sparks that ricocheted between her and Zach. "Gonna have to wait. Got something I need to show you two."

She and Zach exchanged looks. How long had Kirk been listening? They followed him across the Smoky Mountain Investigative Force's lobby. A huge buck hung over the fireplace, his antlers decorated with ballcaps Kirk had collected from the parks he'd worked. A fire crackled in the hearth. In the carpeted conference room, the projector screen lit the room in a dull blue, reflecting off the buttery, oak-paneled walls, until Kirk pressed play on a connected laptop.

"We have a problem."

Jimmy Vern Buchanan's face flashed on the screen. Annalise sucked in a breath. Cody Moss's kidnapper—SMIF's first case.

"You remember he pleaded for a lesser sentence?"

Annalise and Zach nodded.

"He's been released."

"What?" Annalise's heart tripped over its own beats. "When?"

"How?" Zach added. "Why?"

Kirk held up his hands. "One thing at a time. I've requested the details. They haven't arrived yet, so all I know is he is out."

"That's ridiculous." Annalise crossed her arms over her chest. "How can anyone let a man who kidnapped and tortured a child out? How could any reason be good enough?"

Kirk shook his head. "I don't know."

"What are we going to do?"

Silence spanned the room for a long set of heartbeats pounding in her head.

"Nothing." Kirk sank into a cushy conference chair.

"Nothing?" she and Zach asked simultaneously.

Kirk lifted his hands and shrugged. "There's nothing we can do. Other than request details, which I've already done."

"Can we at least keep an eye on him?" Zach asked.

"From a distance only," Kirk replied.

"That's gonna be hard to do. The only way to see into his farm is to be on his farm." Annalise joined Kirk in the chair opposite his.

"Exactly." Kirk slid a folder across the table. "This is an exact map of his property boundaries. Since it does back up to the Great Smoky Mountains, if we needed to, we could get that close." He pointed to a location at the corner farthest from Buchanan's cabin.

"And we can't see a thing other than trees and field," Zach said.

"So what do we do?" Annalise asked.

"Wait," Kirk answered. "And hope he behaves."

"Awesome." Zach sat next to Annalise and patted her hand, resting on the tabletop.

Kirk swallowed hard and tapped the folder. "There's more."

"What?" The look on Kirk's face sent Annalise's stomach churning.

"We have a new case."

"Oh." She opened the envelope and stared at photos of a body lying at the bottom of a cliff. "Who is it?"

"Jake Zucker," Kirk began. "He was on a trip with his family at Spence Field. They woke up this morning, and he was gone. They found him like this."

"How old is he?" Annalise asked.

"Seventeen."

Zach tightened his grip on her hand. "Where'd the photos come from?"

"The father snapped pictures on his phone before he ran back into Cades Cove and flagged down a park ranger."

"Interesting," Zach said.

"I thought so too."

"Okay, let's grab our gear."

"Hang on, Annalise." Kirk leaned back in his chair. "You know how happy I am to see you two together. But—"

"But what?" Zach said.

Annalise squeezed Zach's hand in return.

"For this case, until I figure out the… logistics of you dating and being partners, I'm going to work with Annalise."

Zach dropped her hand and rose to his feet. "You can't be serious."

"Zach, you will be working with Oliver Tobias."

"Oliver Tobias is in Middle Tennessee at the training center."

Annalise rose next to Zach and placed her hand on his forearm. "It's fine, Zach. It makes sense." And it did. They had discussed the possibility of this, at least at first until everyone saw they could work together as a couple and not lose their edge.

"I'm aware, Zach. You're going to drive out and pick him up. He finished the academy today."

"What then? Sit here and wait?"

"Then, you two are on loan to Chattahoochee."

"Georgia?" Zach asked.

"Yes. Georgia."

"What's in Georgia?" Annalise asked.

"I have a friend there. He called and asked for some help. They've had a string of vandalisms."

"Vandalism? Really?" Zach began pacing the distance between desk and door.

"Zach," Annalise whispered.

He spun. "Isn't that a bit of a waste of our abilities?"

Kirk rose and planted his palms on the desk. "It's good PR. It's a good opportunity to show Oliver Tobias the ropes now that he's here on an official capacity. Do you have a problem with my orders?"

Zach squared his shoulders and glared at Kirk. "No, sir. I'll get my brush and dish soap and be right on it." He stormed out of the room and slammed the door behind him.

Annalise smiled. "I'm sorry about that, Kirk."

"Not your place to apologize for his attitude."

True. Zach had been improving over the last few months, but he still had a long way to go in the grieving process it seemed. "He doesn't like the idea of not being there in case I get into trouble."

"And I understand that. But I've made up my mind." He grinned. "Besides, it will give me a better chance to see my agent at work firsthand."

She shrugged. "Not much to see."

"You're too humble, Annalise."

"Thank you, sir." Her confidence had come back, not as strong as before but, certainly, a vast improvement. Her daily prayers and positive self-talk were helping. She shifted her stance. "Well, I guess I'd better get my gear."

"And your thick socks. It's as cold as a polar bear's nose out there."

She chuckled. "Aptly put."

"I try. I'll meet you at the truck in ten."

She nodded and left the office. "Zach!"

"In here." His low voice resonated from the lobby.

She made her way into his office and shut the door behind her. Wait. Would it look wrong for her to be alone with him at work like that? She sighed and opened it again. "It's fine, Zach. I'll be okay."

He hung his head. "I know. It's just…"

"Last time I worked a case without you I almost got killed."

"Exactly."

"We're putting all that in the past, remember?"

"I remember."

She wrapped her arms around his torso and laid her head on his chest. "We knew this was a possibility."

He kissed the top of her head. "But it's worth it so I can call you mine."

She blushed. "Exactly."

"Okay, I will go get Oliver Tobias and head to Georgia. No more complaints."

"And I will hike into the freeze line with my thick socks and help this family find closure."

"And everything will be fine."

She looked up into his face. "Pray with me?"

"Of course. Lord, please protect Annalise and Kirk. And keep their toesies rosy."

Annalise giggled.

"Help them find out what happened to this boy. Watch over me and Oliver Tobias too. Give us guidance. Oh, and keep Buchanan on the straight and narrow, please. We don't want him to hurt anyone else. Amen."

"Amen." She rose onto her tiptoes and kissed Zach's cheek. "I love you."

"I love you too."

A cloud floated over the sun, transforming the luminescence of the office to shadows. Annalise shivered. Thick socks, indeed. And her lined Carhart and padded gloves. And an extra layer of armor around her heart. Everything *would* be fine, wouldn't it?

Chapter Three

Zach stopped at the curb in front of his mom's house, hopped out, and strolled up the concrete walk. How his mother managed to manicure dormant plants into welcoming arms, he couldn't fully understand. As long as he could remember, she'd managed to accomplish just that, and even found ways to add subtle colors with yellow and orange mums, red and white poinsettias, and glittery blue snowflake lights along the sides. He swung open the stained-glass front door. "Hey, Mom!"

"In here, son!" She answered from the direction of the TV room.

As he closed the door behind him, colored sunrays danced through the glass onto the wood floors. After strolling down the short hallway lined with family photos, he poked his head through the doorway. "I'm headed for Georgia. Just wanted to see how you are before I go."

She held her hand out. "I'm fine. But thank you for thinking of your dear old ma."

"You're far from old." He took her hand and kissed the top of her head. "You call Annalise if you need anything. She'll be in town."

Her eyebrow rose. "Trouble in paradise?"

"Nah. Kirk wants to send me and Oliver Tobias to help an officer in Georgia. He needs Annalise to work a new case here." He hated it even more now that he'd had to say it out loud. *What if Annalise got hurt while he was gone? What if another crazy serial killer held her hostage or another drug dealer held a gun to her head? What if Kirk couldn't keep her safe?*

"Out of your head, son."

He smiled. "Yes, ma'am." If only he could. Everything with his dad a few months before and his own injury and then Annalise's close call had led to an endless spiral repeated on high volume: Overthink everything. Everything. All the time.

"Better get on the road, eh?" She winked.

"Yes, ma'am. Love you."

"Love you too, son."

He stepped onto the sidewalk and froze. The hairs on the back of his neck stood on end. What in the world?

Slowly, he took in his surroundings. Quaint houses in a quaint neighborhood with sleeping gardens and sidewalks and ordinary things. Cars in driveways. Frozen puddles. Clear blue sky and wispy clouds. Nothing that should be causing this terrible feeling of being prey.

After a few more moments of inspection, he rubbed his neck and got into his vehicle. He drew a deep breath and attempted to calm his heart rate. Time to get on the road. He looked forward to seeing Oliver Tobias and spending time with his new friend. But, boy, was he gonna miss his long-time friend being his co-pilot.

Annalise leaned and looked again at the boy's mangled body waiting at the bottom of the cliff. Arms and legs bent at unnatural angles. Her eyes closed as her heart screamed. His poor parents! *Lord, please help them.*

She pulled her attention to the campsite waiting behind her. No immediate signs of a struggle glared. The bare vegetation waited silently for spring. The impenetrable stone left no room for footprints or scuff marks. It waited, untouched, since Jake's parents ran down the mountain for help. Two small tents, one for Mr. and Mrs. Zucker and one for Jake, stood in bright red contrast to the winter-dimmed landscape. She peeked inside the parents' tent and found two sleeping bags, a flashlight still shining its dull beam on the thin wall. An overstuffed backcountry pack lay forgotten at the head of the dark green sleeping bags.

Annalise stretched purple latex gloves onto her hands and opened the backpack. She pulled each item out and laid it on the floor of the tent, then photographed the entire scene and each item. Nothing spoke of abnormality.

Inside Jake's tent, she found a sleeping bag and a hiking pack that looked identical to his parents' gear. His bag held fewer items, but still nothing suspicious. A small fire in a rock circle smoldered to ash, one tendril of smoke rising gently from the center of nearly-black embers. The family's foodstuffs hung from a nearby tree at the proper height and distance from the trunk. Annalise stood outside the camp and surveyed the area. She crossed her arms over her chest and frowned. They'd done everything correctly. Yet, their son died. What had happened in the pitch black of night?

"How're we going to get down there, Kirk?" She nodded toward the cliff's edge.

Kirk stopped his periphery search and set his backpack on the ground to unzip it. "With these." He removed rappelling equipment and grinned.

Her stomach clenched. "Oh boy."

"Come on. You've got this. And I've got your back. Or your belay line, I guess."

She took a deep breath. Renewed Annalise, not the scared, broken one, stepped forward.

"Okay." She mustered courage she didn't feel. Slipping on her harness, she prepared her line and backed to the edge. How long had it been since she'd dangled over free air and hoped manmade ropes held? *Lord, help please!* She breathed deeply and blew out slowly. "Ready?"

Kirk nodded. "Ready. Set. Go."

The first step over the edge stole what breath she'd just tried to gather. But the second one made her grin. Dangling over an infinite abyss of death had always given her such a rush. Okay, not infinite. And hopefully not death. For her anyway. Had this kid, Jake, chosen to leap from this height knowing what the end result would be? Did he fall in the dark? Could he have been pushed?

Before she knew it, her feet touched the spongy ground at the base of the cliff. Strewn with leaf litter and damp from the slow drips of water off the rock face, every step lifted an earthy, wholesome aroma into the air.

She unhooked her harness. Kirk lowered a backboard. She laid it on the ground and then belayed for Kirk as he descended. Once he stood beside her, she approached the boy's body. Her joints ached as she took in the odd angles his arms and legs had been contorted into. Had he died instantly? Annalise certainly hoped so. They scoured the perimeter, working in concentric circles inward toward the victim.

There was nothing out of the ordinary, until the center where Jake lay.

"Think it was an accident?" Annalise asked as she kneeled next to the body.

"I don't see anything that says otherwise. But, of course, the autopsy may tell us more."

She stared at the vacant eyes that reflected the crisp sky overhead. He'd never see their beauty again. Such a waste of a young life. Her gaze fell to his cheeks and traveled the contours of his face. He'd been a handsome kid. Sharp jaw line, shaggy hair that seemed to be the trend for teens these days, and clean shaven. She'd bet he had all the girls swooning.

What was that behind his ear? A bug or leaf or something? She leaned closer. A tattoo? Of a whiskey bottle. She gasped.

"What is it?"

"Kirk, look. She pulled the boy's earlobe gently forward. Do you see what I think I see?"

"The Moonshine Mafia."

She blew out a harsh breath. "Is this enough to go see Jimmy Vern?"

"Maybe."

"Maybe? Come on, Kirk! How can you stand there and say 'maybe? You know what he's capable of!"

"Annalise, calm down."

She crossed her arms over her chest. "This is calm."

"You know as well as I do some bigger powers than little ole SMIF are at play. We must tread lightly."

"Tread lightly, my foot. I'll show them tread lightly. When I plant my boot in—"

Kirk chuckled. "All right. All right. Ease up. We don't know anything yet. Not concretely. Let's get him to the medical examiner and go from there. Okay?"

She sighed. "Yes. Okay. But, if this turns out to be related to that monster, I will personally see to it that he never sees the outside of a jail cell ever again. I don't care who or what he knows."

"Deal. If the evidence proves it's him."

"Did you find Jake's cell phone?"

Kirk shook his head.

"Odd. He's seventeen. I guarantee he had one."

"Maybe Mom and Dad wouldn't let him bring it on their family trip?"

"Maybe." No teenager would willingly leave his phone. She made a mental note to ask the family when they interviewed them.

An hour later, after photographing every square inch at the base of the cliff and collecting virtually no evidence, they carried the backboard between them, laboring under the weight of the surprisingly heavy teen. There was no beauty in the shimmer of leftover frost hiding in the shadows nor enjoyment in the purifying, frigid mountain air. Not when their burden was a young boy who'd left too soon. Not when his family waited for his body so they could cry over his coffin and mourn their baby boy.

Chapter Four

"Oliver Tobias, man, it is so good to see you." Zach clapped his friend and new temporary partner on the shoulder. "And congratulations on both items."

Oliver Tobias blushed and ducked his head. "Thanks."

"When's the wedding?"

"May."

"Awesome." Zach unlocked the truck with the remote. "Hop in."

"What, you're not gonna let me drive?" Oliver Tobias grinned.

"Nah. Can't let you start thinking you're in charge of this team already."

The two men chuckled and slid into the cab.

"Chattahoochee, here we come." Zach threw the truck in reverse and jumped on I-24 South.

Every mile he left behind pulled on him. Leaving Annalise wasn't supposed to be in his plan right now.

Three hours later, Zach pulled into the ranger headquarters in Chattahoochee, Georgia, and killed the engine. He sighed.

"You okay?"

Zach faked a smile. "Yeah."

"What do they have for us anyway?"

"Graffiti." He climbed from the truck and slammed the door behind him. He flexed his hand, stiff from driving, and tried to remember some of his low-key PT exercises. Annalise would have been proud.

Oliver Tobias joined his side. "Really?"

"Yep."

"Exciting stuff for my first real SMIF case."

Zach snorted. "Right."

"Well, we all have to start somewhere, I suppose."

The door in front of them flew open. Blu stepped out, and Zach groaned. *You've got to be kidding me.*

"Zach! Good to see you, buddy." The former Cades Cove ranger smiled like he'd just rekindled an old friendship. After his last flirtatious encounter with Annalise, the dude could jump off a cliff for all Zach cared.

"What are you doing here?"

"Requested a transfer. They granted it last week."

"Splendid."

"Right? I needed some help. Had two other officers moved out and they have yet to be replaced. I knew I could count on Kirk to send y'all."

"I'm less than thrilled. Why do you need help with a graffiti case? How could it possibly be that important?"

Blu wrinkled his brow. "They're defacing national treasures, Zach. Of course it's serious."

Zach resisted the urge to roll his eyes. Behind him, Oliver Tobias coughed. "Which national treasures, Blu?"

"Some of our famous bluffs along the river. Hop in, we'll drive out."

"Well, that's just awful. Hey, have you met Oliver Tobias? He's our new trainee."

The two men shook hands.

"It's not what you'll expect, fellas. Rather disturbing."

For the first time, Zach's interest piqued. Just barely. With his transfer, Blu was not going to be anywhere near Annalise again. Maybe this day wasn't going to be so terrible after all.

Oliver Tobias and Zach hopped into Blu's assigned ranger's truck. Blu turned down a bumpy dirt road and half an hour later, pulled to a stop next to the slow-moving river. The emerald waters shimmered under the sun's rays, reflecting bare branches and a blue sky dotted with marshmallow clouds. A frigid breeze whispered in from downstream, and Zach shivered. It'd be a bad day to end up in the icy water.

"Come on." Blu gestured to a canoe tied to a shrubby tree.

Zach raised an eyebrow as he glanced at Oliver Tobias, who shrugged.

Blu tossed two lifejackets their way, then threw his own on and zipped it. "Don't fall in."

Zach bit back a snarky comment. He'd been doing a lot of that lately. His mind seemed like a darker alleyway than it had before his dad's death—before Annalise had to shoot his father—before his own injury and stroke... just before. When had cynicism become his go-to method of looking at the world? He shook his head to clear the thoughts and stepped into the front of the canoe, ahead of Oliver Tobias in the middle and Blu in the rear.

Blu took a few strokes, then paused. "Oh hey, Zach, I hear congratulations are in order. You and Annalise are officially a couple. That's great."

Huh, maybe he'd been looking at Blu all wrong. He nodded. "Thanks, man."

"Sure thing. Okay, if you'd grab that front paddle and help me get us upriver, I'd appreciate it."

Zach did as Blu requested and dipped the blade into the river. The burble of the river reflected off the bank, and the echo magnified the sloshing of his paddle. As he pulled, frigid water splashed onto his hand. Who on earth would brave the icy river this time of year?

The three men swung the canoe around a sharp bend and, waiting before them, there stood a sharp limestone bluff covered in intricately colored artwork.

Zach stopped paddling. What were all those shapes? He squinted. As if suddenly projecting from the rock face, the artwork took on a life of its own. Horrid renditions of men in monstrous masks raised weapons against blood-covered children. Jagged angles and strange shadows played with the lighting to bring the scene awake in the sunlight. Icicles dripped from above, casting a glossy finish over the entire mural. What on earth? Who? Why?

"Told ya," Blu said quietly.

"What do you think it means?" Oliver Tobias asked.

If only Annalise were here. Her naturally insightful thoughts would help clarify the muddled questions rampaging his mind. "I dunno. But it can't be good."

"Dr. Howard, how are you today?" Annalise extended her hand.

Dr. Mason Howard shrugged and raised his bloodied gloves with a smile. A shock of dark hair fell over his right eyebrow. Eyes the color of a newborn fawn sparkled from beneath.

"Oh, right." Annalise lowered her hand.

"I'm doing well, Agent Baker. I haven't found anything yet on this fellow that is out of the ordinary for the circumstances."

She nodded.

"Cause of death is blunt force trauma to the head, presumably from the fall. He also has multiple contusions, broken bones, and lacerations. All suffered during the fall, as well."

"How can you tell?"

Dr. Howard pointed at several deep purple bruises overlying obvious bone breaks, then lifted a lock of Jake's hair to reveal a dark red chasm on the back of his scalp. "Each of them is developed at the same rate, indicating they happened simultaneously. He died within minutes of impact."

"You mean he could feel—" Annalise shuddered.

"Possibly. It is unclear how much the brain can process when the victim is unconscious."

How should she respond to that? The poor boy!

"There's no indication that this was anything other than a horrible accident, Agent Baker."

"Thank you, Dr. Howard. Let me know if you find anything else." Annalise sighed. If only she could believe the friendly ME, but something deep within recoiled at the thought of closing this case file stamped *Accidental*. The tattoo behind Jake's ear couldn't be a coincidence. She spun back to face the body. "What about—"

"The tattoo?"

"Yes."

"I've pulled a file up on my computer there. Please feel free to peruse it."

Annalise walked to his desk in the corner and smiled at the soft hues of a sunset hanging above his computer. She moved a small silver Tree of Life statue to the side and swiped the mouse to wake the desktop. She scrolled through a list of similar tattoos found on various victims for the last fifteen years. Each tattoo resembled a type of whiskey bottle.

"How many are there?" She whispered half to herself and half to Dr. Howard.

"Forty-six since 1994. Mr. Zucker here makes forty-seven."

"You're sure his tattoo fits this group?"

"Positive. It has the correct initialing in the corner."

"What?"

"Come, look."

She returned to the table where Jake's body lay, stiff, waxen-looking. Hard to believe just a few hours prior blood had coursed through those veins. Lungs inflated, the heart beat in a seemingly healthy boy.

Dr. Howard hovered a lighted magnifying glass over the tattoo under Jake's ear. "See?"

Annalise squinted. Faint letters revealed themselves in the corner of the bottle: MM. *Moonshine Mafia*. Her blood instantly boiled, like drops of water thrown into a preheated cast iron skillet.

Images of Cody Moss's boyish face flashed in her mind. Just a year and a half earlier, Jimmy Vern Buchanan, ringleader for Moonshine Mafia, had held the boy captive, starved him for a week, and threatened to kill the boy's mother and Cody himself. How on earth had that monster been released from prison? It made no sense. They had the man dead-to-rights for kidnapping, assault and battery, and a smorgasbord of lesser crimes.

"Thanks, Dr. Howard." She grabbed her cell phone and dialed Kirk on her way up to her Jeep. "It's the Moonshine Mafia," she blurted as soon as he said hello.

"How sure are you?"

"Absolutely positively."

Kirk's sigh echoed loudly through the line. "What do you want to do?"

Annalise stopped midstep. What did *she* want to do? Kirk was their boss, and her partner right now. Shouldn't he be deciding? Besides, what she wanted to do wasn't professional. Or legal. "Go get him."

"Do you have enough evidence to seal his case. For sure, forever?"

Yes! wanted to spring from her tongue, but she couldn't honestly say it. "I don't know."

"That's not good enough." He paused and spoke more softly, "And you know it."

"Yessir. I do." Anger fizzled away, replaced with simmering frustration. "We need to know how Buchanan got out of jail first."

"Yes, ma'am."

"How do we do that?"

"We talk to Brit."

Annalise sank into her driver's seat. "Who?"

"A friend of a friend over at the District Attorney's office. I had forgotten she worked there until I ran into her at the gas station earlier. I happened to drop Buchanan's name. Her face turned red, and she looked like she was ready to explode. I think she'll tell us, whether she's supposed to or not, why he was released."

"I'll meet you there."

Kirk chuckled. "Where?"

"Um, well, wherever you tell me."

"I'll see what I can arrange. Sit tight."

Ugh. One of the things she stunk at: waiting. Especially when it involved Jimmy Vern Buchanan. Her very first case. SMIF's first victory.

She snorted. Right. Victory. Until the DA, or someone with some serious clout, decided to just let the monster walk. She slammed her palm into the steering wheel. How could this happen?

The phone ringing with an incoming video call made Annalise jump. "Zach! Hi!" She grinned at his somewhat grainy image.

He returned her smile. "Hey, beautiful. How's it going?"

Her smile fell. "Not great at the moment. How about you?"

"Blu works here now."

"No way. Really?"

"Really. And I need your help."

"Okay, shoot."

"Hang on, let me send you the pics."

Zach's face disappeared from view, and her phone dinged several times with incoming messages. She opened the first photo and gasped. What in the world? She scrolled slowly through the next dozen. They were disturbing but beautiful in their artistry. The details on the rock faces blew her away. She leaned back in her chair. "In order to spend that much time creating these out of spray paint, someone would have had to rappel and dangle for a very long time in front of that cliff. Do you suppose that's why they did it during the winter? Less likely to be caught?"

"Hmm. I hadn't thought about that. But, yes, I'd say you're right."

She closed the images and once more grinned at his matching smile on the screen.

"I miss you, Lise."

"I miss you too."

"Oliver Tobias is a great partner, but he's not as pretty as you."

She giggled. "Kirk is a great partner too, but he's not as handsome as you."

He shook his head. "All right, give me your professional opinion on these."

"They're amazing."

He chortled. "Okay…"

"The detail is incredible for 'graffiti,' don't you think?"

"That's true. But, Lise, don't you think there's something very wrong with this person? The images… they're… grotesque."

"To a degree, yes. But they remind me of something. I can't quite put my finger on it."

Zach leaned forward and put his elbows on his knees. "Something from an old case?"

"No, something I saw once. Maybe in an anthropology class in college? I'm not an art expert, by any means, but there's something about these. They aren't just some random kid sketching. There's a message here, an importance to them."

"I just need to know who to send the bill to."

She laughed. "Blu's really up in arms on this one, eh?"

"He thinks it's the crime of the century."

"He takes great pride in his work, Zach. That's a good quality."

Zach frowned. "I suppose. And it's a great quality for him to have in this state, not that one."

She rolled her eyes. "Stop it. You know Blu and I are just work friends. Not even friends. Acquaintances."

"I know. I'm just teasing."

"Well, stop. And get back to work."

"Slave driver."

She grinned. "I love you."

"I love you too. Let me know what you figure out on this one, please."

"I will. I'm headed back to the office. Let me do some research and I'll call you back a little later."

"Deal."

An hour later, seated at her desk, Annalise stared at images of ancient demons. Winter sunlight streamed through her window, casting an odd luminescence to the images on her screen and highlighting the oranges and reds even more starkly. The drawings on the computer from an old text, written in Latin and German, eerily matched the current rock art Zach had sent her. As she stared into the red eyes of a half-beast/half-man on the cliff face, a chill crept up her spine. What message did the artist intend to send? Why this particular spot? Did it hold significance or simply convenience?

Someone knocked on the door, and Annalise looked up from her work. "Hey, Kirk. Any word from her yet?"

"Honestly, I think she's blocking my calls at this point."

"Great." Annalise frowned. "Why would she do that?"

"I don't know, unless I really touched a nerve mentioning Buchanan. She probably suspects that is why I'm calling, even though I didn't specifically say that in the three voicemails I left."

"Maybe she's just busy?"

He shrugged. "It is court day in Knoxville today."

"Maybe she's the paralegal on a big case and is stuck there then."

"Maybe. Have you heard from Zach?"

"Yeah. Come look."

Kirk came to Annalise's side of the desk and leaned in. "What is that?"

She showed him her phone. "Photos of the 'graffiti.' Interesting, eh?"

"Gives me the creeps."

"They are very macabre."

"You could say that."

"I don't know how they plan to catch the culprit, though."

"Only one way to catch a graffiti artist."

"How's that?"

"Wait for them to come back."

"This looks finished. Why would they come back?"

Kirk pointed at the corner of the cliff face closest to the river. "Empty canvas."

"Brilliant."

"Thanks." He grinned. "I'll let you know if I hear from Brit."

She nodded. Before he was fully out of her office, she'd dialed Zach and said hello. "Kirk's so smart."

"Well, yeah, that's why they pay him the big bucks."

"I heard that!" Kirk shouted from the hall outside her doorway.

Annalise chuckled. "The artist is going to come back."

"How do you know?"

"Kirk pointed out that there's still empty space. Ask Blu if this all appeared overnight or if it happened a little at a time."

"Okay, hang on."

The line fell quiet other than faint echoes of voices in the background that she couldn't make out. Zach came back on the line. "It took a couple weeks. But this time, it's been over a month since anything new was added."

"Oh. So Blu already thought of that?"

"Sort of. He said each time they noticed something new it was because a kayaker or canoer had come in and told them, but they hadn't made it out themselves till Blu arrived because they've been so short-staffed."

"It's time for you and Oliver Tobias to have your first stake-out."

"It would seem so."

"You can introduce him to the Zach method."

"Oh yeah. Just have to decide what to bring."

She chuckled. "Good luck. Keep me posted."

"Will do."

Annalise hung up and leaned back in her chair. Zach's case might be solved soon, but what about hers? Out there somewhere, Jake Zucker's murderer waited in the shadows, and Brit might have important information about it. Annalise couldn't afford to just sit and hope the woman grew a conscience and called Kirk back. She had to do something.

Chapter Five

Annalise checked her phone for the tenth time in three minutes. How had it only been three minutes? She sighed. No one had come out of the courthouse recently. The doors would be locked by now at fifteen after six. Had she somehow missed the crowd coming out of court? Or was it just running really late? Hopefully, the latter. And, hopefully, Brit was indeed here. Kirk had described her as a petite blonde. Much more than that, and Annalise had to trust God to give her a nudge about the woman holding answers about Buchanan.

She paced in front of her Jeep for another ten minutes, watching the afternoon traffic crawl by on the narrow, old streets of downtown Knoxville. The leftover cobblestone streets caught the tires differently, sounding like a strange clock ticking as they crawled for home. She checked her phone again and resumed pacing.

Around the corner, famous Market Square offered savory temptations. Her stomach growled. If it would be much longer, Annalise could stroll over and grab fried chicken and waffles with sweet tea. Maybe distract herself from the waiting. She shook her head. Sheesh. She was starting to think like Zach, always about food. She missed him. Kirk hadn't said how long Zach and Oliver Tobias would be on loan to Georgia.

Things had just started to feel normal again between her and Zach. After she'd shot and killed his father, she could feel the resentment radiating off Zach for weeks. And after he'd been injured and had the stroke, the frustration he felt about his physical inabilities only added to the strain between them. But for the last four weeks or so, things had started to feel good again.

The front doors finally swung open. A man and woman stepped out. The man's voice drifted over the rhododendron-lined courtyard, and the woman laughed loudly. Annalise briskly approached the couple moving away from her. "Brit?"

The woman spun on her pointy heels. "Yes?" The woman's face drained of all color. "I can't—I'm not supposed to—"

"I just have a couple questions. Please, ma'am."

Brit backed up a couple steps.

The man in his dark gray suit and salt-and-pepper hair at her side took her elbow. "Who is this, Brit? Are you okay?"

"I'm Special Agent Annalise Baker. I just need to talk to her for a minute. It's really important."

Brit shook her head. Her large eyes shone with fear, but the shorter woman took a deep breath. "Agent Baker, there's a gag order on this matter. I can give you no information. Period. Do not ask again."

"But—"

"Gregory, give me a minute."

The man hesitated but then stepped away several feet.

"Agent Baker, I really cannot divulge any details."

"Jimmy Vern Buchanan is not a good person. How could your all's office just let him go?"

Brit pressed her pink lips tightly together.

"He tortured a kid, for crying out loud!"

"We're aware. I think you'll find that Mr. Buchanan has… given invaluable information in exchange for his freedom, and that freedom may be short-lived."

Annalise opened her mouth to speak. Wait. What did that mean? "I don't understand."

"You're not the only one looking to pin Mr. Buchanan to the wall, so to speak. You, Agent Baker, should watch your back too. There're more parties involved in this than you realize.

Some may be closer to you than you can imagine."

Close? What did that mean? A chill rocketed up Annalise's spine as Brit scurried away.

Zach pulled his Carhart tighter around his neck and shivered. "Cold out here, ain't it?"

From somewhere in the darkness to his left, Oliver Tobias answered with a grunt.

The sun would be up in about an hour, and they would be there, waiting to see if their graffitist made an appearance. If the person happened to show up, they'd be ready. The chances were slim, but better than sitting in Blu's headquarters all day listening to him elucidate the honorable history of America's national parks.

The stars had started to fade, but in the humidity-free air, each one stood out like a string-light. If only Annalise snuggled next to him, with their body heat mingling and their lips... He shook his head. He couldn't let that thought go any further. Not yet. Not until...

Until he proposed?

He'd certainly considered it, in passing. But it seemed like such a stretch. How could his best friend since childhood have become the love of his life? How could he be so blessed? *Thank you, Lord, for the blessing of Annalise.* He raised his weaker arm. It felt more normal than even just a week ago. He was making progress physically. The nightmares about his father had slowed too. Maybe it was time? They'd only dated for a couple months, but he'd already loved her a lifetime.

The sky above him took on a purplish hue at its eastern rim. Slowly, it changed to peach, bright pink, then orange. Finally, the golden orb appeared through the bare tree limbs on the horizon. Streaks of gold burst between the trunks, highlighting dark leaf litter on the hillside. *Gorgeous. The graffiti artist has got nothing on you, God.*

"Stunning," Oliver Tobias whispered.

"Yeah, man, it is."

"I don't think he's gonna show up today, do you?"

"Nah. But ain't that sunrise worth the numb toes?"

Oliver Tobias chuckled softly. "Good point."

"Besides, we have the cameras to put out, so it's not a wasted trip."

"That's also true."

"How's Corinne doing, Oliver Tobias? How is she really?"

Oliver Tobias maintained silence for so long, Zach doubted he'd get an answer. When he did, his voice vibrated with unshed emotion. "She struggles. The things she went through... she still has nightmares, but—and she feels badly saying this—she's much better off than poor Helene. At least Corinne escaped before that…" Oliver Tobias' voice had hardened when he spoke again, "monster could hurt her worse than he did."

"How did she escape? Did she ever remember?"

"One of the great mysteries of my lovely fiancée."

"One of them?"

Oliver Tobias laughed. "She's had an interesting life. Traveled a lot. I have a feeling that we'll grow old together and I'll still be hearing new stories."

"I'm happy for you, man." The dusky morning made it easier for him to address his emotions aloud. "I hope Annalise and I will get there soon too."

"Y'all have been through a lot in recent months. But I see the way you look at each other. There's no doubt in my mind this is His plan."

Zach certainly hoped so. He had misunderstood his father's role in his life since his teenage years, and that resentment spilled over when Henry died. The blame didn't lay in Annalise's lap. He needed to show Annalise how much he had moved past all the bitterness over his death, to show her how he was never mad at her in the first place.

"I can't feel any of my body, Oliver Tobias. Come on. Let's put these up and go get breakfast."

"Sure thing, partner."

Oliver Tobias meant it lightheartedly, but it stung a little. He wanted Annalise back by his side. Forever.

His plan. Zach's words tumbled in Oliver Tobias's mind as he climbed into his hotel bed and dialed Corinne's number.

"Hey, babe," she said in a sleep-tinted voice after three rings.

"Hey, gorgeous. Sorry I woke you."

"I wasn't asleep. Well, I sort of was. Not completely."

He chuckled. "You're a terrible fibber."

"I'm glad you called. How's it going?"

"Slow. Not what I expected."

"I'm sorry." She sighed. "I miss you, Ollie."

He grinned. Strange—coming from her— Ollie didn't sound so bad. "You know you're the only one I let get away with giving me a nickname, right?"

"So you've said. Several times."

Sergeant Myers had ruined nicknames for him. The man's ugly, square-jawed, red-cheeked face flashed into mind. He breathed back the anger that accompanied the man's implanted memories. "I miss you too, pretty lady."

"When are you coming home?"

"Not sure. We're trying to catch this guy in the act. Could be a few more days."

"What about the tux fitting?"

He groaned. "I'm sorry. I completely forgot. Can we reschedule it?"

"Of course."

He sensed no irritation in her voice. No hurt. Nothing but support. Warmth burrowed even further into his heart. *His plan*. Indeed.

Chapter Six

Annalise planted her palms on Kirk's desk and leaned toward him. Photos of his wife and daughter lined the edge near her left arm. Awards and photos of Kirk jumping out of planes, climbing mountains, and dangling out of helicopters hung on the wall behind his chair. "Hear me out, boss." Heavy cloud cover threatened snow, but she couldn't let it deter her desire to get outside and on Buchanan's trail. "We have to go up on the mountain, just at the edge of his property line, and watch him. That doesn't break any rules. If we stay on national land, we'll still have a good view."

Kirk took a swig of his coffee. "I dunno. Something's telling me it's too soon."

"He's dangerous. Someone should be watching him."

"We don't know the details of his plea bargain, of his release."

Annalise may not know details, but she knew the look on Brit's face. And she knew something awful headed their direction. "Kirk, I'm talking stake-out. Nothing more."

"Looks, and smells, like snow."

"We've got winter gear. We'll be fine."

"I'll think about it, Annalise. Go file the rest of the paperwork from last week's missing hiker."

They'd found that missing hiker less than a hundred feet off the Appalachian Trail with a sprained ankle. She'd have the paperwork finished by lunch. If Kirk didn't think quickly, she'd have to find something to do with her energy.

Ten minutes of working at her desk later, her office door swung open and smacked into the wall behind. Kirk strode in, his face flushed red. "You talked to Brit? Without me?" He crossed his arms over his chest and planted his feet hip-width apart.

Annalise shrank into her chair. Had she ever seen that look on Kirk's face? He'd been upset with her, sure. But this? The impulse to run nearly overtook her. She nodded slowly.

"We talked about you going out on your own. Remember?"

Again, she nodded. Memories of all those arguments with her ex-husband flooded her. Of the way he acted as if Annalise held all responsibility for every problem they had. Never mind he'd cheated. Made her feel worthless. Tears pressed into her eyes. Hadn't she worked through all these memories? Apparently not. "I'm sorry, Kirk. I got impatient. Everything Cody Moss went through can't be for nothing." A tear escaped, and she brushed it away with angry swipes. "You and I both know Buchanan deserves to be in prison for the rest of his life."

The look on his face softened as he released his arms. "You and I both know that, yes." He closed the door behind him and sat across from her.

She scooted her chair backward.

"Annalise, this is bigger than us. Okay? Me trying to scare you off it isn't working. Will me pleading with you to be patient help?"

He knew something. Of course! "Level with me, Kirk."

"This doesn't leave this room."

Her stomach bottomed out. She placed sweaty palms on the desk and scooched back in. "I promise."

"Buchanan turned on the Moonshine Mafia. He's planted on the inside to help roust out the new ringleader that took Zach's father's place."

Pressure, like a fist slamming into her, rocked her stomach. "But that doesn't make sense. The two gangs aren't related."

His right eyebrow lifted toward his slightly receding hairline. "They are now."

"How do you know all this?"

"I told you I'd talk to Brit."

That's how he knew about her indiscretion as well. "I'm sorry, Kirk. You know I respect you infinitely. This case—It just—Buchanan is a snake."

He smiled. "It was your first case with SMIF. And you have become quite attached to the Moss family."

She nodded.

"It's been a rollercoaster with Zach's injury and his father's death. Are you sure you didn't come back too soon?"

Fire ignited in her chest, replacing the leaden boulders of moments before. Did she rush into talking to Brit because her judgment still needed improvement? She pressed her eyes closed and pictured Buchanan's face. No fear sprang to the surface, only a gust of injustice and the need to right it. Immediately. "I didn't make a mistake. I acted on the information you gave me. Did I go about it wrong? Yes. Did it need to be done? Yes. Give me the word, and I will go stake his place out alone, if need be. You know it needs to happen."

He nodded.

What intimidated him so much on this one? Had someone gotten to him besides Brit? "This red-tape bureaucracy isn't how we do things here, Kirk. We do what needs to be done to get the case closed. Period."

"You're right, Annalise. You're absolutely right."

"So I can go?"

"No."

Her heart sank. "What?"

He grinned. "We can go."

Her smile instantly matched his. "Excellent."

"But, and this is a big but, we have to be extremely, incredibly, acutely careful. Do you understand that this must be airtight and exactly by the book?"

"Got it, boss." She mock saluted. "When do we leave?"

"Go get your winter gear." He glanced out the window. "There'll be fresh snow on the mountains before nightfall."

Zach waited in a plush leather chair. In the corner of Blu's new office, Zach massaged his neck with his stronger hand. That hotel bed made him wish he was home.

The cabin that housed the Chattahoochee National Forest Park Rangers held the warmth from a hearth fire like an oven mitt. Nestling the soft glow within thick, hundred-year-old logs. A nest cradling them in its belly. As he focused his attention on the flames dancing amid the old fireplace stones, his body succumbed to the relaxing crackles and pops. He could see why

Blu left Cades Cove and its modernity. A man could learn to love this place. Blu put in long hours just like he and Annalise and Kirk did. A cozy office like this could ease that burden.

His phone pinged with the new sound he'd set, alerting him to an incoming photograph from their game camera. He snapped to attention and yanked it from his pocket. As he opened the app, it dinged three more consecutive times. He entered his password. The images popped open. He clicked on the first thumbnail.

"Blu! Oliver Tobias!"

He sprang to his feet and met them as they burst through the front door.

"What is it?" Oliver Tobias asked.

"Zach?" Blu said.

"Look." Zach held his phone out, as three more alerts sounded. "He's there right now."

A ponytailed man with a bright orange rappelling harness and wearing a backpack lowered himself down the cliff.

"Let's go get 'im," Blu said as he grabbed his keys off the peg by the door.

They jumped into Blu's SUV and raced for the canoe entry point. None of them spoke as they donned their lifejackets and grabbed the paddles. Zach's heart pounded. He hadn't expected to care this much. Fifteen or so minutes later, they rounded the final bend and a grin spread on Zach's face. The man dangled there, spray-painting the empty space just as Kirk and Annalise had predicted. "Gotcha."

"Well, whaaddya know," Oliver Tobias said.

"Great work, guys." Blu picked up a bullhorn.

"Wait!" Zach hissed. "If this man is an experienced rock climber, he can be up that cliff and out of here way before we can. If you announce our presence, he's gone." For that matter, the guy could see them sitting in the canoe and bolt. "We'd better get out of sight quick too."

Oliver Tobias dipped his paddle in the water and pulled hard. A few strokes later, before Blu or Zach could put action to words, they were hidden behind a thick rhododendron grove on the bank.

"Okay, Zach, this is your baby now," Blu whispered. "What do you have in mind?"

Zach flexed his weaker hand. It didn't hurt any longer. He pressed his shoulders back and smiled. "There a way to get on top of that mountain, Blu?"

"Sure thing." Blu climbed out of the canoe, tied it to the trunk of a rhododendron, and motioned for them to follow.

At the base of the cliff, Zach tapped Oliver Tobias on the shoulder. "Stay here?"

Oliver Tobias nodded.

Zach and Blu made their way around the southern edge of the cliff face and began a steep climb upward. No maintained trail awaited them.

Blu became a mountain goat finding all the nooks and crannies needed. Zach watched Blu carefully and used the same hand- and footholds. They wove between oak, pine, poplar, and hemlock trunks, wild grape vines, and various leafless bushes.

Annalise had been right all along about Blu being a good guy, hadn't she? *Lord, give me the words and the courage to set it right.* He took a deep breath. "Hey man, I know this is a weird time. I need to say something to you."

"Okay, shoot."

Blu didn't slow his ascent, and Zach was glad of that. "I've been unfair to you."

"How so?"

"I thought you liked Annalise and had been hitting on her. I judged you wrongly. I'm sorry." Weight lifted from his chest.

Blu chuckled. "Is that all?"

Zach felt a smile break across his face. "Whaddya mean, is that all?"

"I've known you thought that from the first time I met you guys."

"And it didn't bother you?"

"Annalise is a beautiful woman, Zach. And she's kind-hearted and driven and strong. You're a blessed man."

Zach swallowed hard. "Yes, I am."

Blu stopped so suddenly, Zach slammed into his back. Blu spun and held out his right hand.

Zach took another deep breath and met Blu's hand in a firm grasp.

"No apology needed, but apology accepted."

"Thanks, man."

Blu patted Zach's shoulder with his free hand and smiled. "No sweat. Let's get this guy. He's messing with my park."

They reached the summit. More out of breath and muddier than when they'd started. Zach once more flexed his weaker hand, felt the strength coursing through it, and smiled. Maybe all those silly exercises had done some good after all. *Thanks, Lord, for healing and for Annalise. She's the best helpmate a man could ask for.*

Blu pointed northward. "Lead the way."

Following the natural curve of the bluff, Zach crept toward the edge that would bring them above their graffiti artist. A few moments later, they emerged from the trees and undergrowth to see a single line stretching from the base of a tree and disappearing over the rocks. He and Blu stopped shoulder to shoulder.

"What now?" Blu asked.

"We wait."

And wait, they did. For over two hours, with Blu napping in the shade and Zach pacing. His thoughts refused to settle. But at least the two activities kept him warm.

As much as he tried to avoid it by forcing them to leave the topic alone, he kept falling back on his late father. His father's nearly lifelong deception rankled. Henry Leebow had left Zach and his mother. Lied to them about the reason for it. Then gone rogue and led a drug ring for years. The whole story stirred nausea and heat in Zach's stomach. Yet, somehow, the searing pain had dulled to a throb. When had that happened?

Oliver Tobias twirled a blade of grass between his thumb and forefinger. Seated on a fallen log behind a boulder, he occasionally peeked out to check the man dangling far overhead. The guy seemed to be in his own world, one filled with art and spray paint and limestone and nothing else.

He tossed the grass aside and stuffed his hands under his arms to warm his stiffening fingers. What was Corinne doing right about now? Probably snuggling with his German Shepherd on the fluffy white couch. Too bad he wasn't there, his head in her lap and her fingers dancing through his short hair. How much had God blessed him with his headstrong, brave, fierce woman?

Lord, you know all she's been through. Help me keep her safe. Thank you for blessing me with her presence in my life.

Corinne had done more in a couple months to help calm his PTSD than years of going it his own had. "Zach spoke more truth than he knew." His words carried away on a cold breeze. But they resonated in his heart. Corinne was saving him from the darkness. Little by little, day by day.

His blood boiled when he thought of all she'd endured. If it killed him, nothing hard would ever touch her again. In a few short months, she wouldn't have to leave him to go home. His yurt, situated in the beautiful Royal Blue mountains, would be their home. Their sanctuary. And he'd watch over her and love her and keep her safe, no matter what came.

A louder noise than he'd heard all day came from the cliffhanger. Oliver Tobias peeked out from his sheltering rock. A can of spray paint lay on the bank of the river, punctured and shooting lime green color into the air in a large arc. Hissing and spinning wildly as the can emptied itself. Oliver Tobias chuckled, watching the man gesture and listening to the curse words flow down the bluff.

The man began to climb. Oliver Tobias stepped closer. When it became obvious the man would make it to the top, Oliver Tobias prepared the boat and waited. Maybe now he'd get to go home to his love.

A noise behind Zach caused him to spin on his heels. The graffiti artist's line shook the tree and rattled the attached carabiners. The guy was climbing up.

Zach tapped Blu's foot. "Time to arrest someone."

Blu's eyes snapped open, and he leapt to his feet. "Ready."

Zach grinned. "This is the fun part, right?"

"Right."

They approached the edge of the monolithic, plateau of limestone and peered over the edge at the same time. The graffiti artist reached up for a handhold, glanced toward the sky, and froze.

"Hi there," Zach hollered. "Come on up. I think we've got something to chat about."

The man's face paled. He looked toward the ground.

Oliver Tobias stepped from his hiding place and waved. "Hey buddy!"

For another few moments, the man hesitated, then he began to climb once more.

Zach sat on a prominence in the rock. "Take your time. We'll be here."

Blu chuckled.

When the graffiti artist's head cleared the edge, Zach grinned. "Welcome back, man."

"I can explain."

"This oughta be interesting."

"I'm an artist. A famous one. See." The man pulled his phone from his pocket and opened a

Google search tab. He typed in Anthony Walls and clicked on images. "That's me."

Blu said, "And your point is?"

"This is a new experiment. Art in Nature, or maybe Natural Art, or even Artscapes... I haven't decided yet."

"You defaced a national park. It's not art. It's a felony," Blu said.

"You're missing the point. It's *art*," Anthony added.

Wow. What was this jerk's deal? Zach stepped closer and grabbed Anthony's elbow. "While it's beautiful," as Annalise had said, "it's also a crime. You're under arrest."

"That's great!" Anthony put his hands in front of him. "All the best artists have been in jail at least once in their lives."

Zach stumbled over what to say, finally settling on, "All right then." They escorted the man awkwardly back down the mountain and into the canoe. Anthony was smiling every time Zach caught a glimpse of his face. Interesting man. He couldn't wait to tell Annalise about all this.

He shot her a quick text and waited to hear the reply notification. By the time they got back to the SUV with their new arrestee, he still hadn't heard anything. "Hang on a sec, guys." He stepped a several feet from the vehicle and dialed her number. It went straight to voicemail.

Odd. A knot formed in his stomach the size of a tomato. Where could she be?

Chapter Seven

Annalise peered at the crystal-clear trail of footprints shining like beacons in the snow behind her. If Buchanan had men out checking for intruders, there'd be no missing them. Annalise shivered. They'd be sitting ducks. She patted her sidearm and blew a breath. *Focus on something else, Annalise.* She couldn't erase the tracks. Perhaps the snow would build fast enough to fill them in soon.

Snow fell in heavy, wide flakes, sifting through the cover of evergreens to land in soft whispers, like satin curtains dancing in a gentle summer breeze. Though it was only a dusting so far, the flakes contained enough moisture to crunch under her boots with each step. The sound reminded her of her childhood winters spent traipsing around the forest with her dog. Both of them silently enjoying the peaceful blankets that fell at least once each season. It never ceased to amaze her how snow transformed the landscape, covering each imperfection in clean linen.

Ahead of her, Kirk slowed and then stopped. He held up his hand to signal halt.

She followed his gaze down the ridge. Buchanan's farm lay in perfect view. Not a soul stirred, but a thin whisp of smoke curled from the chimney. That same cabin once held a teenage boy prisoner in its belly. Too bad she couldn't race in there—guns blazing—and finally bring Buchanan the justice he deserved. *Sorry, Lord. I know vengeance is supposed to be yours, but this man—you know how much of a devil he really is.* Annalise unclenched the fist she hadn't known she'd made. It wouldn't do for her to go rogue here. She had to play by the rules and get something new on this jerk. Something he couldn't wriggle out of.

Kirk slid his pack off and sat on a log. He pulled binoculars from his bag and pressed them to his eyes.

Annalise crept to his side and took a seat next to him, pulling a long swig of water from her bottle as she did. "See anything?"

"Movement in the cabin. Can't tell who or how many."

"Good. Means he's probably there."

"I'm going to move closer. You stay here."

"You sure that's a good idea, Kirk?"

"We're still a couple hundred yards from the Smoky Mountain boundary. What's he going to do? Have me arrested for trespassing on public land?"

"You know he's capable of much worse than that."

Kirk smiled. "Just trying to lighten the mood. I'll be right back."

For a guy who had argued the merit of this endeavor so strongly, he sure did disappear closer toward danger quickly. In less than three minutes, Annalise had lost sight of him, and her heart migrated to her throat.

A strong wind started over the mountains to her left, roaring as it caressed the treetops, like a wave riding the tips of their branches. She heard it long before she felt it, and when it did finally lift the stray strands of hair that had escaped her olive-green beanie, she shivered.

A gunshot pealed out somewhere below. Annalise ducked for cover, landing flat on her stomach behind the log. Where had that come from? Kirk's gun? Buchanan's? Deep shouts rose on the air and filtered up the ridge. More shots belted out, breaking the illusion of safety that had come with the silence of the snow.

Annalise slowly unholstered her weapon and checked to verify a round waited in the chamber.

Behind her a footstep crunched on the snow. Her breath froze in her chest. She blew it out slowly and risked a quick peek above the log. A deer, perfectly silhouetted against the backdrop of white, stood not ten feet away. She sighed.

More angry shouting drew her attention to the glade below. Three men stepped into the opening, one gesturing wildly with a gun-clad hand. She grabbed her binoculars and peered through them. Buchanan stood on the front porch of the little cabin, his rotund form stretching tight a denim shirt and a cigar dangling from lips over a long brown beard. It bobbed as he spoke.

She moved the lenses to the men in the yard. Two she didn't recognize held one between them she did.

Kirk.

The color of his face matched the new-fallen snow. His lips remained pressed together. Wasn't he going to say anything to plead his case? Come on, Kirk, say something.

Annalise watched a moment more, then tucked the binoculars in her pack and rose to her feet. She had to help him!

The man to Kirk's right raised a gun behind Kirk and slammed it into the back of his skull.

Annalise stopped and clasped her hands to her mouth to prevent screaming. No!

Kirk crumpled to the ground. Both men pounded Kirk's limp body over and over, kicking him, slamming the gun into his head, punching him repeatedly.

Annalise's shaky legs refused to hold her without aid. Her heavy arms reached in slow motion for a nearby tree trunk. Was this really happening? From this distance, any bullet she fired would fall short. *Think, Annalise!*

No course of action made sense. No plan could save him. Anything she did would result in the men rushing up the ridge toward her. She watched in horror, a helpless statue, as they beat him to a pulp.

After what seemed like an eternity, the men stopped and backed from Kirk's form. Blood stained the white in clear contrast, growing larger and darker like an ink blot on rice paper. He didn't move. Even without the binoculars, Annalise could tell his body was lifeless.

Bile rose into her throat. She clamped her hand to her mouth once more, but the vomit came anyway. She fell to her knees and retched until her abdomen ached. Hot tears dripped into the snow, melting tiny divots. She had to get to Kirk. Or she had to get away and get help. She had to do something! Her body refused to listen to her commands to rush down the hill and rescue Kirk.

Would help be too late anyway?

A succession of three shots rang out from below. On autopilot, Annalise rose to her feet and sprinted in the direction of SUV parked on a muddy backroad a mile or more away. She never looked over her shoulder. She couldn't.

He'd been following Annalise and the other officer for days. Since he'd managed to send Zach to Georgia, calling in a favor or two and pulling some invisible strings, he had one less person to keep alive. Annalise had made that job infinitely harder since she'd decided, apparently, to come take a looksie for herself at the situation with Buchanan.

Henry, hidden well behind a rise in the ground covered in thick brush, watched the scene unfold below, a knot forming in his throat. *I can't go in closer without giving away my existence. No one can know yet, but I can't help from this distance. Why didn't I bring the rifle?*

He drew in a long slow breath as the men below started in Annalise's direction. They stopped and gathered in a knot of angry words and gestures. *If I don't do something, she'll be dead too. What can I do?*

Henry rose from his haunches and skip-hopped closer using trees for cover. The men below still seemed to be gathering their wits, pointing up the hill toward where Annalise was watching only moments before. They seemed unsure which direction she had fled. One of them grabbed the dead officer and dragged him into a dilapidated building. Blood stained the snow in his wake. *Now's my moment.*

Henry fired several shots their direction, aiming but knowing the bullets would never find their target at this distance. The shots echoed off the insulated landscape. The men turned and immediately returned fire. Henry flattened his back against the tree, counted to five, and ran up the mountain. He knew they'd be watching for movement. *Hopefully, they'll follow me and not her.* He had to protect the love of his son's life.

Zach ended the call after four rings and put the phone on the corner of Blu's office desk. Why could he still not get in touch with Annalise? And where was Kirk? Had something happened in the Buchanan case? His stomach churned.

Oliver Tobias caught his gaze from across the room. He tilted his head to the left.

Zach mouthed, "I'm okay."

Oliver Tobias nodded.

But Zach's mind looped through every what if, bad-case scenario it could think of. Twice.

He forced his attention back on Blu's efforts to process Anthony Walls. The local sheriff's department awaited his arrival, as soon as Blu could discern a semblance of explanation from the man. He'd been trying for three hours. Zach had been resisting the urge to tell Blu to give up for two and a half.

A hand clamped on his shoulder, and Zach jumped. He spun and found Oliver Tobias close to him. "Man, don't do that when a man's lost in thought."

"You're not okay."

Zach shook his head.

"Annalise?"

"And Kirk. I can't reach either of them."

"We caught the graffitist. Let's go home."

Duh. There was no reason for them to wait. Why had that not occurred to him? He signaled Blu across the room, and the younger officer nodded. Soon, he was flying up the interstate for the Tennessee line.

Shadows grew longer, casting jumbled gray streaks across the yellow lines. The radio playing soft country oldies made the only noise above the hum of the tires. Yet, Zach's mind whirled as fast as the rubber. Something was wrong. He could feel it. Annalise would never ignore his calls for this long, never leave her phone off unless she was out of service. And if she was out of service range, she was in the mountains somewhere. Without him.

"Look out!" Oliver Tobias grabbed the dash with both hands.

A leather-colored blur appeared from his left. He crammed on the brakes too late. The sickening sound of flesh smacking metal filled the cab. Quick. Crunching. Metal bending. Always louder than he expected. His truck slid to a stop. He glanced in the rearview and saw the deer lying in the middle of the northbound lane. Poor critter.

Steam poured from under his hood, hissing at the wild injustice of being turned into an exit for his coolant system. Great, just great.

He limped the truck to the shoulder, turned on the flashers, and finally remembered Oliver Tobias's presence in his passenger seat. "You okay, man?"

"Yeah. We oughta move her."

They exited the truck simultaneously and walked in silence to where the doe lay. Each of them grabbed two legs and hoisted her into the bed of his truck. Zach scanned the tree line where she'd darted out. No other deer waited for her. They'd either run or she was truly alone. It seemed silly for a grown man to worry about her herd, but he felt guilty for removing her from the equation in such a horrific way. What a waste it was.

Oliver Tobias popped the hood while he studied on the deer's familial situation. The sound of the hood latch brought him from his stupor. "Guess I need to call a tow truck, eh?"

Oliver Tobias's voice came from under the lifted hood. "Yep. This radiator ain't gonna hold antifreeze ever again."

"Lovely."

"Easy fix, once it gets to the garage."

"Right."

Oliver Tobias slammed the hood shut. "May be a reason for this delay, Zach. God knows what He's doing."

What reason could He possibly have? He needed to get to Annalise.

Slow down, Zach. He felt God speaking to his heart in His usual calm, quiet manner.

I'm scared, Lord. Zach exhaled deeply. *Protect her. And Kirk. Please, God. We can't lose anyone else.*

For the first time in a long time, a keen sense of missing his father washed over him. As he stood there on the side of I-75, leaning on a busted truck, staring at a busted deer, tears filled his eyes. He missed his father. Not hated him, not wanted to hit him upside the head. Missed him. Missed the man he'd been when Zach was young and they were passing the football in the front yard or he was handing his dad wrenches in the garage. Missed the way his Old Spice lingered on Zach's bedsheets after his goodnight hug. *God, I don't understand why You had to take him before I could reconcile with him, before I could understand the truth of his situation and his job and the sacrifices he made for Mom and me. Why couldn't You let me make peace with the man before he died?*

The question hung in the infinite empty space between Zach and Heaven. Seconds ticked by that felt like days. A single teardrop fell and splattered on his knuckles.

With the next breath Zach drew, peace washed home, filling his heart like impregnable fog. He may never understand it all, but God had good reason. And that was a good enough why.

When he lifted his head, Oliver Tobias stood across the truck bed from him, how head bowed in what Zach knew was silent prayer. A barely audible "Amen" reached his ears. Zach smiled. What a good friend Oliver Tobias had turned out to be. And not a bad partner either.

Cars zipped by while they waited. Zach covered the doe with a tarp and tightened ratchet straps over the unfortunate form. If only they could harvest some of her meat, he'd not feel so badly. It would be too bruised.

An hour later, a tow truck arrived and loaded his truck onto its bed. He and Oliver Tobias hopped into the cab with the driver. Mike, his name tag said. Mike drove them to the nearest auto shop and unloaded them in the parking lot. After paying Mike, Zach surveyed the mom-and-pop venue.

A white-haired, stoop-framed man whose denim jumpsuit read "Piston" emerged with a clipboard and a smile. "What can I do ya for, young'un?"

Despite the anxiety swirling in his chest, Zach couldn't help but smile. "Hit a deer. Not too worried about the dents, but I think a new radiator would be awful helpful."

"Shewwww, they're bad out here. Can have it fixed for ya, though, in two days. Takes a day to get the radiator and hoses in." The old man spit a stream of brown tobacco juice onto the dormant grass.

Zach frowned. "You can't do it any faster?"

"Sorry, young man. Best I can do's two days."

"Is there a rental agency anywhere nearby? I've got to get home. Like yesterday."

Piston scratched his whiskery chin. "Not that I can think of. S'pose ya could call your insurance and request one from Chattanooga, if ya was so inclined. Prob'ly be tomorrey 'fore they could get it here, though."

Zach growled. Tomorrow wouldn't be good enough either.

"Trouble at home, young man?"

"We're special agents with SMIF," Oliver Tobias piped in. "Our coworkers aren't responding to our texts or calls. We're a mite worried."

"S'that so?" Piston dug in his pocket and retrieved a set of keys. "Take Jolene. She ain't the purtiest, but she'll get ya there."

"Jolene?" Zach said.

Piston tossed Oliver Tobias the keys and pointed to the left of his shop. "Built 'er myself."

Zach renewed his frown. "We couldn't possibly take your personal vehicle, sir."

"You said you's in a hurry. There's yer solution." Piston spat another perfect stream and wiped his chin with the back of his hand.

"You're sure?" Oliver Tobias asked.

"As a heart attack. Just get 'er back to me once you know your friends are all right."

Zach grasped Piston's hand in a firm shake. "Thank you. You have no idea how much I appreciate this."

"No problem, young man. No more deer, 'specially not in my Jolene. You hear?"

"Yessir." Zach considered saluting but thought better of it and instead hurried to the light blue pickup and hopped in the driver's seat.

Oliver Tobias jumped in passenger and handed him the keys. "Want me to drive?"

"Nah. I'm too anxious to sit there with nothing to do."

"Have you checked with Milt?"

"Tried calling and texting him. He responded about twenty minutes ago with, 'Will look into it.'"

"Helpful."

Zach knew Annalise's mentor, former captain, and friend Milton Brooks would dig as hard as he could, and if there was information to be had, Milt would find it. "Could be."

Out of the corner of Zach's eye, he saw Oliver Tobias's head dip.

"Thanks, man."

"For what?"

"Not pushing too hard." Zach smiled. "Being here."

"Where else am I gonna be? They're my team now too, ain't they?"

Chapter Eight

Annalise skidded to a stop and bent over to catch her breath. Her hands pressed into shaking knees. In the fading light, her exhales puffed into the cold air in dark mini-clouds. How far had she run? It felt like miles. But was it far enough?

The forest sat in silence, heavy as the snow. Blanketed in the newness of the white overlay, what little light remained in the sky provided enough clarity for even small details. Like the fact that no birds flitted or squirrels skittered. Or the fact that snowflakes still fell and shushed softly through the branches while her heartbeat pounded so loudly she feared even the sleeping mountain could hear it. She had to keep moving.

Annalise stood erect and slowly took in the details of her surroundings, forcing her breaths deeper into her chest, willing her heart rate to slow. West swallowed the sun behind her. That meant the truck should be to her left. Somewhere.

A breeze picked up stray hairs that had broken free from her ponytail. She shivered as they tickled her neck. She had to get out of there. Fear prickled her thoughts, yet her feet refused to move. They were coming. No doubt about it. She was one of those loose ends on television. They'd killed Kirk. They'd kill her too.

Kirk!

She'd just left him there, lying in the snow-covered mud. Blood mixing with orange clay and—

Dizziness stopped her spinning thoughts and forced her to focus on her physical state. It grew darker every second she wasted. Colder too, with the wind picking up steadily the farther toward night that time traveled. She had to make a plan.

She and Kirk had chosen to pack lightly. Their plan hadn't included gunshots and running and murder.

Though not ideal, she grabbed a handful of snow from a branch and ate it. Her body temperature would drop if she consumed too much, but thirst took priority.

The cool moisture woke her dulling senses. She took a step forward in the direction she believed the truck waited. The crunch echoed like a gunshot off the silence around her. Surely, Buchanan's men could hear her footfalls. Better to go slowly and stealthily? Or simply bolt again and try to outrun anyone who may be back there?

An invisible force pushed at her back, but she refused to give in. Slowly and stealthily would ensure she didn't get lost even worse in the rapidly dimming light. She patted her sidearm again. If worse came to worst...

Darkness arrived faster than she'd hoped. Soon, sloth was her only available pace. With the thick cloud cover and the still-falling snow, she was encased in a coffin and buried alive above ground. Three feet became her best visibility. Years of experience searching for lost hikers screamed in her mind. Stay put! Conserve energy! Wait for help to arrive.

None of those mantras took into consideration the gang of thieving, murderous thugs potentially following her.

She needed a convenient rock shelf to hide under like in *The Lion, The Witch, and The Wardrobe*. And for the person chasing her to be a kind, robust-bellied ally. She chuckled mirthlessly. Kirk was dead, and no one was coming to rescue her.

Annalise stumbled over something in the dark. She pitched forward and caught herself with her outstretched hands. Pain zinged into both elbows. Ice-crusted snow swallowed her face, tiny freezing darts piercing her skin. She had to stop. She righted herself and fumbled in the dark for whatever she'd fallen over. A log as big around as her torso materialized. It would have to do.

She dug handfuls of snow out, creating a depression to sink her body into. With stiff fingers and numb toes, she pressed her back against the log and lay still. At least, hopefully, they wouldn't be able to spot her if she refrained from having a fire. But, in the morning, they might find a human-sized ice cube frozen to the dead tree.

Zach and Oliver Tobias rolled up in front of SMIF headquarters just before ten p.m. and slid to a stop on the snow-covered asphalt. Kirk's vehicle sat cold in the parking lot. The vice-like grip that had ahold of his chest tightened a notch or two.

Zach leaped from the truck and raced to the door. He unlocked it and darted immediately to Annalise's office. Waiting on top of her desk, Annalise's thick trail-map binder sat opened to a section of Great Smoky Mountains National Park he was all too familiar with. One half of his brain sighed in relief.

"Bless you, dear woman!" He stepped back into her doorway. "Oliver Tobias! They went to find Buchanan!" Saying it aloud made the second half of his brain race in frantic circles.

Buchanan was capable of pure evil. If Annalise… He swallowed, hard.

Oliver Tobias emerged from Kirk's office empty handed. "How do you know?"

"My girl left me a clue." He held the binder up. "She's been collecting and making trail maps since she was a young officer. She's created one of Buchanan's place. Left it opened to that page."

"Okay. Good. First thing in the morning—"

Had he heard his friend correctly? He scrunched his eyebrows together. "Not morning. Now."

"Zach, it's freezing. The roads are a disaster. They haven't even had a chance to scrape or salt anything."

"Exactly."

"Exactly what?"

"Annalise and Kirk are out there in this mess. If they're hurt—if they're underprepared at all—they'll not survive till morning."

"When was the last time Annalise was underprepared for anything?"

True. But still. His heart thudded against his ribcage. "I can't wait." He pushed past Oliver Tobias and aimed for his office. Inside, he began gathering supplies, yanking his hiking boots, heavy gloves, and thick coat from the closet and piling them on his desk.

Oliver Tobias followed, pausing in Zach's doorway. "Zach. You're no good to anyone getting hurt looking for them."

Zach slammed the closet door shut. He spun to face Oliver Tobias and pinned him with a glare. "If that monster still had Corinne, would you wait?"

Oliver Tobias's shoulders sank as he exhaled. "No. I get it." He sighed. "I've seen worse odds than these. Let me get my stuff."

"You don't have to come." His tone held as much bite as the air outside.

"Wouldn't dream of staying."

Zach nodded. Good. He could use any help he could get. They hurriedly packed and threw the gear in Oliver Tobias's truck. Zach couldn't risk taking Jolene even higher into the mountains and their slick roads.

"You'd better drive," he told Oliver Tobias as they finished packing the gear. "I won't be able to slow down enough."

Oliver Tobias simply nodded.

Zach bounced his knee the entire hour and a half drive, stopping only once to text Milt and tell him the news. He didn't notice road conditions or stop signs or curves they might have slid around. When they arrived at the parking area and saw Annalise's Jeep, he nearly shouted. He'd been right. Her map was a clue. She was out there somewhere. He and Oliver Tobias just had to find her.

They donned their winter gear in silence. Zach tossed a backpack containing emergency supplies over his shoulder and started into the edge of the forest. He studied the ground under his headlamp for evidence of tracks, but the snow had wiped it all clean.

He glanced at Oliver Tobias. "Anything?"

"Nah. Too much snow."

Annalise and Kirk had entered from the same direction they'd used when investigating Buchanan originally. Zach snapped a photo of her map and returned to the truck to leave the binder. "Look at this map, Oliver Tobias." He pointed at a corner of the screen near his left thumb. "This is where I'd enter, here." He gestured to the forest, where his and Oliver Tobias's tracks dotted the edge of the trees from a few moments before.

Oliver Tobias nodded.

"And I'd follow this general direction around and park above the cabin to get a good view."

"I'd agree."

"Okay, then that's where we go." He took a few moments and programmed in coordinates to his phone's GPS. It probably would lose service at some point but worth a shot. His stomach tied in knots as he faced the pitch-black, frigid forest. *Lord, where is she? Please guide us.*

Zach's boots sank into the now-foot-deep snow with loud crunches. He wrestled each step free to prepare for the next. In a few hundred feet, he labored for breath. At this rate it would take all night. Soon enough his thighs screamed for rest, but he continued to push. Behind him, Oliver Tobias never uttered so much as a groan. No wonder Annalise had fought for Oliver Tobias to join their team. He was made of steel, had a heart of gold, and faced evil with a fist of iron.

Zach checked his phone. He'd lost GPS signal but the time showed they'd been hiking for an hour. He pulled his compass from his pocket and used it to double check their bearing. They were still headed in the correct direction.

"Zach, look."

He whipped his head up. "What?"

Oliver Tobias pointed at the sky.

The snow had stopped sometime since they'd left the truck and a full moon peeked between fingers of wispy white clouds. As he looked bac to the forest in front of him, for the first time since they'd begun he could see clearly past the arc of light from his headlamp. He switched it off, and the world around him lit up like a sparkling vanilla-frosted fantasy. Moonlight bounced off the snow everywhere he looked. He could see as well as sunrise or set.

He picked up his pace, ignoring his burning legs. Another hour and a half passed as if they were mere minutes. Startled, he drew to an abrupt stop. "There," he hoarsely whispered.

Buchanan's cabin had manifested out of the landscape as if by magic. Sitting like a dark skull on a brightly lit slope. Zach shivered.

No lights shone from within. In fact, nothing looked alive anywhere. *Where are you, Annalise?*

"I'm gonna get closer," he whispered. "Stay here."

Oliver Tobias shook his head. "On your six, Zach. Just be careful."

They drew their weapons and crept closer. Oliver Tobias's footsteps behind him matched Zach's so closely they sounded like one entity. At the door of the cabin, Zach held his breath and paused to listen. Absolute silence.

He pushed on the front door. It creaked loudly as it swung open. Still, nothing moved inside. Oliver Tobias gripped his right shoulder and squeezed, then released. Zach swallowed and stepped through the black door. He immediately pressed his back against the wall to the right of the door and waited. *Patience, man.*

He counted to three and then slid his feet silently sideways five paces, until he felt an obstruction blocking his path. He knew Oliver Tobias would be on the opposite side of the room doing exactly the same thing.

Again, he counted to three and then switched on his headlamp. Oliver Tobias's strained face illuminated across from him. No one else waited in the one-bedroom cabin.

He blew out a deep breath. "Check for anything that might help us figure out where they went."

Oliver Tobias flipped on the cabin's overhead light and cleared the bathroom and single closet.

Zach froze. The basement crawlspace where they'd found Cody! He bolted out the door and around the side of the cabin. He threw open the doors and raced down the damp stairs. "Annalise?"

No one replied. The dank, dirt-floored area sat empty. Memories of Cody's rescue just two years prior threatened to flood him. He shoved them aside.

"Zach!" Oliver Tobias's voice filtered down the stairs.

"Be right up!" He stomped to the top and frowned. "She's not there."

"I found something. Come on."

He followed Oliver Tobias back into the cabin.

"Look at this." Oliver Tobias held up a scrap of paper.

Halfway up the ridge behind the house. East.

Zach shuddered. Why did the handwriting look so familiar? Not Annalise's, but who did it belong to? He couldn't put his finger on it.

"What are you thinking, partner?"

Zach tore his gaze from the paper and met Oliver Tobias's. "Could be a trap."

"Could be."

"Could be a clue."

"Only one way to find out."

"That's my line."

Oliver Tobias chuckled. "I know." He clapped Zach on the shoulder. "Let's go get your girl."

Warmth filled Zach. God knew what he was doing when he sent Oliver Tobias into their lives. He swallowed and nodded. He'd never heard a better idea.

Chapter Nine

Annalise awoke with a start. What was that noise? She pried her eyelids open with great effort and blinked a couple times. Why was it so bright? Surely morning hadn't yet arrived. Turning her head to look at the sky proved a challenge. Her core body temperature must have been so low. She had to move again. Had to figure out how to turn sludge back into blood. How to warm stiff muscles refusing to listen to her brain's slow commands.

"Get up, Annalise," she whispered. *Get up!*

Her abdominal muscles shook as she righted herself. Pain shot into her legs and arms. *So this is what it feels like to freeze to death, eh, Lord?*

She took a moment to gather her bearings. The full moon had escaped its cloud prison while she slept. With it reflecting off the thick snow, she had no trouble seeing every tree, standing or fallen, now. She massaged her biceps, one after the other, then rubbed some friction heat into her thighs.

She took a step. A gunshot rent the peaceful night. Annalise's knees buckled. She caught herself on a tree trunk. Her heart rate skyrocketed. Pings of pinching pain ricocheted in various parts of her frigid body. Thoughts coagulated and got stuck trying to exit their synapsis. What was she supposed to do? Where could she hide? Running would not be an option, unless she wanted to faceplant again. And now darkness wouldn't be shielding her.

Up would be too hard. Which way was the truck? Annalise grabbed the sides of her head with her gloved hands. *Think. What are you doing?* Robotically, she turned and headed down the mountain. Maybe in the crevice between she could find a hiding spot.

A shout floated to her through the clear air. A man's voice. If they were close enough to hear…

Annalise picked up her speed, half-walking, half-sliding down the steep incline. Her numb feet didn't seem to want to do what they were supposed to do. Her boot caught on something buried in the snow, and she tumbled forward. Her body rolled, her mind powerless to stop it. Snow, sky, snow, trees. She slammed into something hard. A moan flew from her mouth. "Oh, ouch."

How were her words so calm when her body screamed in pain? Who was she even talking to?

Her eyes fluttered closed. Rest beckoned to her from over the hump of exhaustion. Her body relaxed. "Just for a little while. Just a…"

"Annalise!" Zach stopped for the hundredth time and listened for a reply. He and Oliver Tobias had been searching for hours. They'd found no disturbed snow. No signs of their presence whatsoever.

"Maybe they've made it back to the truck by now?" Oliver Tobias stopped a few dozen feet away.

Maybe. What did a situation like this require? He shoved the emotions aside and tried to think rationally.

More help. A better plan. A helicopter. A dog team.

His shoulders slumped. "Let's head back and regroup." He fired one last shot. "Annalise! Kirk!" And waited for several minutes. Once the echo of the gunshot faded, silence met them. Either Annalise and Kirk couldn't hear them or—

"Come on, Zach. Let's get more resources."

Zach's feet remained rooted in place. "I can't just leave her."

"We're not giving up. Just trying again."

"What if—"

"Don't go there yet. Not yet."

The lump in his throat made swallowing difficult. He nodded and turned back toward Buchanan's place. *I'll be back, Lise. Soon as I can get more help.*

"Corinne, baby, I am so sorry I keep calling and waking you up." Oliver Tobias paced the parking lot in front of SMIF headquarters, slipping in the crunchy snow every few steps.

"It's fine. What's wrong?"

Corinne's mom spoke in the background.

"It's Oliver Tobias, momma… I don't know… I'll come find you in a minute, momma." She paused. "Sorry. I'm back. Momma's worried about you. Said her mom instincts are tingling."

He choked on the emotion rising in his throat. "Annalise is missing."

"Missing?"

"Out there. In this weather." He swallowed. "Corinne, she's… It could be real bad."

She drew a sharp breath. Her voice trembled when she spoke. "Did someone… Does someone have her?"

His stomach dropped from under him. "Oh, Corinne, no. I'm an idiot. I didn't think. She's lost. We think, anyway." How sure of that were they? The body in the shed. The men in Buchanan's gang. The possibility existed.

"I know one thing. Annalise is the toughest fighter I've ever seen."

"Not the toughest." He chuckled. "That title belongs to my girl."

She laughed. "God got me through this far, Oliver Tobias. He'll get Annalise through too."

"You used my whole name."

"The occasion called for it. Don't get used to it, handsome."

All these years, he'd insisted on the respect forcing people to use his whole name garnered. As soon as he'd climbed ranks high enough, he'd always introduced himself with both his first and middle names. Special Forces turned the respect into a family bond. He hadn't been able to let that feeling go.

"Ollie? You still there?"

He smiled. "Yes, ma'am."

"What's the plan?"

"We're rounding up four-wheelers and helicopters and a team. Heading back at dawn."

Silence reigned the line for several long minutes.

Softly, he spoke again. "I wish I was there."

"I wish you were too."

"I'm scared, Corinne." He'd never admitted that aloud to anyone. Ever. "Seeing Zach, knowing I know exactly how he feels."

"Not exactly. You didn't already love me when I was missing."

He smiled. "No, that's true. But I can empathize." He swallowed again. "I'd be dying if I was in his shoes, Corinne. I... I don't think I could stand it."

"Hush, and listen." She cleared her throat. "Nothing like that is ever going to happen to me again. I'm safe. And," she paused, "I am so proud of you."

"For what?"

"For admitting your fear. It takes a strong man to do that."

He huffed. "Or an extremely weak one."

"Once a soldier, always a soldier. I think even more highly of you than ever before."

He couldn't find the words to respond.

"I love you, soldier."

"I love you, too."

"Go get Annalise. I'm praying you forward."

Dawn broke in a pure blue sky. Sunlight streamed through the windows of SMIF's headquarters, but for the first time the homey office brought Zach no comfort. No sense of safety. Only the profound loss of his best friend, the stark emptiness of her office, and the hole growing in his heart.

At 6:07, Milt burst through the front door wearing a scowl, followed by two officers wearing Norris Police Department uniforms. "What's the holdup? We should be out there."

Zach shook his hand. "We're waiting on the helicopter team to tell us when they're going. No cell service."

"Use the radios!"

Zach bit back a smartalec response. Milt loved Annalise like a daughter. The man's fear had to be as big as Zach's. "I've got them in the truck already, Milt. We're champing at the bit too." Champing at the bit was putting it mildly. It would be far more accurate to say ready to smash heads and plow down entire national parks if that's what it took to find her.

The office phone rang. Oliver Tobias, seated closest to it, answered it on the second jingle. He spoke softly a few quick words then hung up. "Let's go. They're on their way. Weather's perfect for flying."

"Did you remind them we think they're east of the cabin?" Zach asked.

"Yes. They'll start there."

"All right. Jasper coming too?"

"He's already on his way too," Oliver Tobias said.

"Thanks, man. Four-wheelers?"

Oliver Tobias nodded. "Blu's got his friends meeting us at the parking area with three."

Great. Why wouldn't his brain focus on lining out the plan? Annalise's beautiful face flashed into mind. What if she was in real trouble? She'd been in danger before, sure. But this felt different. He'd never been unable to reach her. Not since he'd stuck up for her in that sandbox. She'd always been there. Always at his side in one capacity or another. Even during their time apart at two different academies, she was his closest friend. He couldn't live without her. Wouldn't want to.

"Zach?"

Oliver Tobias's voice shook Zach from his zone-out. "Huh?" Everyone stared at him. "Right. Let's go."

The drive back to where Annalise's vehicle waited passed quickly. Before Zach knew it, he stepped from the vehicle into the snow and geared up.

A young officer approached him and handed him keys to a four-wheeler waiting nearby. "I'll follow you, sir. Your partner here can take the third."

"Great." Zach took the keys and hopped onto the ATV. *I'm coming, Lise. Just hold on.* Over the ridge to his right, the fwip-fwip hum of a helicopter manifested and grew louder. A few moments later, it zipped overhead, swirling snow down on their heads. In its wake the empty branches seemed almost sad to be free of their adornment.

Zach pressed the gas and raced after them. He thought the officer and Oliver Tobias followed somewhere behind him, but he honestly couldn't be sure. Nothing slowed him. When he popped into the glade surrounding Buchanan's cabin, he slammed on the brakes and skidded to a halt. Took a deep breath. And scanned the sunlit landscape for any clues. His and Oliver Tobias's footprints shone like black eyes. Nothing else appeared out of place.

"Where are you?"

Hallucinations. Had to be. Annalise's eyelids fluttered open to blinding sunlight streaming through the thick hemlock she'd managed to somehow collapse under.

Or had she? Hadn't she been lying in the open only a few moments before?

When had dawn arrived? When had the snow stopped? Nothing in her head made sense. She squeezed her eyes shut. *Think, Annalise.*

When they fluttered open again, a man's form approached her. None of her extremities seemed terribly concerned. Certainly, not enough so to make her rise and run.

His voice drifted to her through cotton balls. Mumbly and thick and nonsensical. She strained to understand.

Why try so hard to understand a mirage? Maybe it was a sign from God?

Maybe it was an angel welcoming her Home.

She closed her eyes again. When she opened them, a flame flickered in front of her face. Licking a small pile of sticks. Even its tiny heartbeat threw warmth onto her skin. Every cell longed to be closer. To dive into its center. She couldn't tear her gaze from its lovely dance.

Green hemlock branches fell onto the tiny fire. It hissed its frustration, then smoke began to billow from the popping needles.

"They'll be here soon. Just hold on a bit longer."

God's voice sure sounded oddly familiar out loud.

Zach swung the door to the storage building open and immediately regretted it. His stomach plummeted to his toes. Was that—

He turned away. Tears streamed down his face.

"Oliver Tobias! Help!"

Oliver Tobias ran toward him, worry written on his expression.

Zach pointed to the bloody body lying in the building. "Oliver Tobias, please. Tell me it isn't…isn't—"

Oliver Tobias's face paled, but he stepped around Zach and looked at the inert form. "It's a man."

"Oh, thank you, God." Zach nearly collapsed. Caught himself on the doorframe. "Is it Kirk?"

"Don't know yet."

Zach radioed it in. "Gonna need the ME."

"Ten-four," Milt answered. Static sounded for several long seconds. "Is it Annalise, Zach?"

"No." He let off the radio button and sighed. "But it might be Kirk."

He spun slowly around and took in the details of the man's wardrobe. Knelt and attempted to look at the jacket's breast area without looking at the badly disfigured head. The torn fabric, discolored by tacky dark blood, matched the one Kirk had hanging in the office.

Zach pressed his palms to his eyes. "I need some air. Come on, Oliver Tobias. We can't stop looking."

He dropped his emotions in the doorway. He didn't have time to think about whose body it was. The ME would figure it out.

A voice crackled over the radio. "Helicopter to ground one. Got smoke, fellas."

Zach's heart leapt. "Where?"

"Northeast."

He scanned the treetops. "I can't see it."

"Hang on." The helicopter swung wide and headed north for a few hundred yards and then hovered. "Here."

Zach peered harder at the sky. From such a low angle, there didn't appear to be anything out of the ordinary. "I don't see smoke. Just trees."

"We're marking it on our GPS. Hold tight."

Zach paced to the four-wheeler, climbed on, and started it. Without a word, Oliver Tobias did the same.

"Okay, guys. Here ya go." The helicopter officer's voice read a string of coordinates to Zach.

He jotted them on a notepad in his phone and then checked them against his compass. He didn't have to look to know Oliver Tobias had his six when he headed into the trees. He stopped every few hundred feet to find a new marker to aim for.

"There!" Oliver Tobias's voice flew to him above the hum of the ATVs.

Ahead, a red smoke flare, like a giant smoke bomb from childhood Fourth of Julys, hissed, discoloring the snow. *They could've picked a better color*. Whoever's corpse lay in the shed would probably not appreciate the irony.

The smell of smoke reached him, kicking his pulse into overdrive. "Annalise!" He stopped and killed the engine to listen. "Annalise! Sweetheart, where are you?"

Oliver Tobias pulled to his side and turned his key off. "Anything?"

"I smell smoke. Still can't see it. You?"

"What's that?" Oliver Tobias pointed to gouges in the snow.

"Looks like drag marks." Drag marks! He burst into a sprint, reaching and then following

~ 93 ~

them around a bulge on the side of the mountain, like a tumor growing from the soil.

A tall hemlock with low-drooping branches sat in the middle of a small glade. The needles brushed the snow with the breeze, tracing tiny crisscross patterns on the surface. Just outside their circle, a small fire nearly smothered under the weight of fresh-cut branches.

"Annalise!"

A small moan reached his ears. His breath froze in his chest. He swallowed and took several steps toward the fire. "Annalise?"

He parted the branches and, there, lying against the base of the tree, covered in a woolen blanket, she waited. Unconscious. Moaning in her sleep. He rushed to scoop her up. "Annalise!" He pressed a kiss to her forehead. "You're cold as ice. Oliver Tobias! I found her!" Plopping onto his backside, he scooped her limp form into his lap. "Oh, thank you, Lord, I found her!" He nuzzled his face into the nape of her neck and let the tears he'd been holding back pour onto her skin. "I love you, Lise. So much."

Oliver Tobias appeared between the branches.

"Get the wheeler!"

The younger officer spun on his heels and disappeared. The four-wheeler's motor putted to life and grew closer.

Tension flowed out of his muscles. They'd found her alive. But Kirk... Where had Kirk gone? Could the body in the shed truly be their boss and friend?

Chapter Ten

Two p.m. Still white-faced and out of it. Would she wake up? What if she didn't? Zach's thoughts had been running in circles for hours. The chopper brought her here and they'd gotten her immediately in a room. Immediately started evaluating. Started slowly warming a nearly-frozen body. Vitals? Stable. Core temp? Stable now.

"Come on, Annalise." He squeezed her hand for the hundredth time. Brushed her hair away from her face. Kissed her forehead. "Wake up. Please."

The door swung open, and Annalise's nurse entered. She smiled warmly. "Any change?"

He shook his head.

"She'll pull through. Just you wait and see."

"I don't know what I'll do if she doesn't."

"Have faith." She checked Annalise's blood pressure and temperature. "Everything's still good, hon. Keep praying."

He tried to smile. Instead, tears pooled in his eyes yet again. As the nurse exited, Milt entered, his cheeks red and his eyes troubled.

"What is it?"

He nodded.

"Kirk?"

"'Fraid so."

"How did he—" He already knew that answer. Kirk had been beaten to death. The image of the mauled, puffy face and broken skin raced over him. The dented, misshapen skull. Nausea threatened to overwhelm his senses. He swallowed, took a deep breath.

"They've processed the place. Found the note you mentioned still on the table, like you said it'd be. No sign of the gang." He cleared his throat. "We have no idea where they went."

"Lovely." The note. Who had written the note? It seemed like a dream. Something unreal. Had one of the men gained a last-minute conscience and betrayed Buchanan?

Milt's gaze traveled to Annalise's peace-filled expression. Tears sprang into the corners of his eyes. "Is she gonna be okay?"

"I don't know. Her core temp was so low when we finally got to her. They say there could be brain damage."

Milt lifted Annalise's other hand and traced the IV. "She's a real special one, Zach."

"I know, sir."

"She has to pull through this. She's the toughest woman I've ever had the pleasure of knowing."

Warmth filled Zach's chest. Milt's father-like love for his girl would bring joy to their lives for years to come. She'd probably have Milt and her father both walk her down the aisle. He smiled. She'd be the most beautiful bride in the history of time.

The door swung open, and his mother entered. "Look who I found."

Annalise's parents rushed in behind her. Zach rose and hugged all three, then introduced Annalise's parents to Milt. "You all got here fast."

"Our baby girl needs us," her mother said.

Her father shook his hand. "Thank you for always being here for our daughter, Zach."

"I want to marry your daughter, sir."

Stunned silence filled the room. Then, as if one unit, everyone laughed.

Annalise's father released his hand and pulled him into a hug. "Your timing could use some work, son."

"I've known you two would be forevers since you were six," his mother said.

Annalise's mom smiled and patted his head, like he was still twelve and hanging out for brownies after school.

The levity of the moment lasted only until they each turned to face Annalise lying inert and unmoving next to them.

Zach chuckled. "Now we just need the bride to wake up so I can ask her."

"Do we know what happened," Annalise's father asked.

"We're putting the pieces together," Zach started, "but until she tells us for sure, I'm not sure we'll know each detail."

"What do we know?" her mother asked.

Zach cleared his throat and took Annalise's hand in his once more. He stroked her ring finger. *Soon.* "There's a case involving a dead teenager. It's tied to a very bad man Annalise and I helped arrest some time ago. We think Annalise and Kirk went to stake-out his place and got caught." He swallowed.

Milt continued the narrative. "It seems that Kirk was murdered by these men. Somehow Annalise escaped but, perhaps in the dark last night, got turned around."

"Or she was hiding," Zach added.

Milt nodded. "Either way, here we are."

Oliver Tobias pulled Corinne tighter to his side. The movie they watched held no interest for him, but she seemed to be enjoying it.

She smiled up at him and returned her gaze to the screen, shoving another handful of popcorn into her mouth.

He grinned. "You're beautiful."

"What? Now?" Her popcorn filled cheeks marred the words.

"Yes, now. And always."

She finished chewing and swallowed. "Thank you."

"Let's get married."

"We already are."

"I mean now."

Popcorn flew out of her mouth. She paused the movie, scooched over, and turned to look at him fully. "What?"

He grabbed her hands, his heart flying out of his chest. "I can't spend another night here without you. I need to know you're mine. Once and for all. Fully. God sent you to me, I know it."

She stared at him with a blank face, eyes wide.

Was she ever going to respond? His breath stuck in his throat.

"Okay."

"Okay?"

"Okay."

He leaped to his feet and grabbed her to his chest. "Let's go."

"Now?"

"Right now."

She kissed his cheek. "Let me get my dress."

"I still don't have a tux."

"Wear those tight Wranglers that fit your backside so well. And your boots."

He chuckled. This woman was going to continue to surprise him every day of his life.

Two hours later, Oliver Tobias smiled down at Corinne as her mom and dad and the minister watched. "You look beautiful."

She blushed. "Thank you, handsome."

The white gown's tiny beads glittered like snowflakes in the afternoon sunlight. Behind her, the canvas shell of their yurt held a myriad of flowers, polka-dotting the tan with red, white, pink, and green. Mom Porter had not hesitated to help with decorations and to make them a small cake, and she now stood alongside Pops Porter and grinned ear-to-ear.

Oliver Tobias nodded at them, and they returned the gesture. Mom Porter swiped at a happy tear.

The minister to his left began the ceremony, and Pops Porter slipped his arm around his wife's shoulder. A breeze kicked up, gently dipping the heads of the grass like an earthen wave of approval.

For the first time in a long time, Oliver Tobias's heart felt truly full. Before he even had time to blink, he was lifting Corinne's veil and preparing for a kiss.

Corinne stood on her tiptoes and whispered in his ear, "What are you thinking, soldier?"

He'd have to tell her later that it was the perfect day in the perfectly intimate setting to marry the perfectly imperfect woman of his dreams. Because the last thing his lips wanted to do was talk.

Zach's head dipped, and he jerked upright. He'd been sitting at Annalise's bedside for twelve hours. His butt was numb and his body, apparently, wanted sleep badly enough to risk him falling out in the floor for it. Annalise's parents and his mom had left just before visiting hours closed, but he'd given the nurse a look that made her instantly close her mouth when she'd asked him to leave. He wasn't going anywhere. Not without Annalise.

He gently scooched Annalise's limp form to one side of the hospital bed, lowered the nearer rail, kicked his boots off, and climbed onto the lumpy mattress next to her. Wrapping his arms around her body, he pulled her tight and stroked her hair. "Wake up, Lise. I know you're in there.

You have to wake up." His heart strained to leave his chest and join with hers a few inches away. She had to wake up. There were no other options.

Soon, Zach's eyelids grew heavy, and his hand fell to the clean white sheet.

Some time later, from somewhere deep inside the recesses of his exhaustion, Zach felt a tug. A gentle pull on his heartstring.

"Zach?"

His eyes flew open. He pulled back and stared into the gorgeous green eyes he'd come to love. "Annalise! You're awake!"

She attempted to smile, but her lips still seemed partially frozen.

"You're awake?" His heart leapt. "You're awake!" He jumped out of her bed, ran for the door, returned to raise the sidebar, and then ran back to the door. "She's awake!" he hollered into the hallway for anyone who may be close enough to hear. Like the parking lot.

Annalise chuckled. "Zach."

He spun toward her. "Yes, my love?"

"I saw something… someone… out there."

He returned to her bedside and took her hand. "There was no one else, Annalise. You were alone when we found you."

She frowned. "Kirk?"

A nurse rushed into the room, momentarily saving him from the answer. The man began double checking vitals.

"I'm hungry," she said.

Zach's pulse fluttered. "That's my girl."

Her lips seemed to have awoken fully, and she blessed him with a toothy grin. "Leave it to you to be so happy I'm hungry."

"Means you're okay."

She blushed. "Oh."

He leaned down and kissed her forehead, resisting the urge to keep his lips planted there permanently. "I love you, Lise."

"I love you too, Zach. What about Kirk?"

Heat scorched his insides. "Annalise... I..."

"It was real then. It was all real?"

"What was, sweetheart?"

The nurse finished and excused himself with a quiet, "I'll be right back."

"The attack. Them beating—" She grasped at the covers, wadding them into her fists.

Zach gently took her hands in his. Heavy weights settled onto his shoulders. "What happened, Lise? Tell me everything."

Annalise fell, landing hard on the snow. It burned her face with scorching heat. Behind her eyelids, blood sloshed, splattering every surface of imagination. Drops flung on white walls. Dark pools coalescing around healthy people. Raining down in huge drops and splatting into her hair.

Kirk's face floated in free-space, red tears running down his face.

She screamed and bolted upright in her hospital bed.

Zach's arms encircled her, pulling her close.

Her entire body trembled at the cellular level. "It was awful, Zach." She buried her head in his chest, closing out the now-dark view beyond her hospital window.

"Sshhh, Lise." He rubbed her back. "It's okay. Just a nightmare."

Her stomach roiled. "That's the problem, Zach. It wasn't just a nightmare. Kirk's dead. And I couldn't help him."

He sounded deflated when he spoke again. "I know."

Annalise sat up and swiped tears from her cheeks with both hands. "There's something else. I keep dreaming about the man who helped me."

"There wasn't a man, Lise."

"Was there a fire?"

Zach nodded.

"I didn't build it. I'm certain of it."

"You must have. Who else—"

"That's what I'm trying to tell you, Zach. There was someone there, helping me."

His brow wrinkled. "One of Buchanan's men?"

She pressed her eyes closed and tried to bring the man's form into sharper focus. She'd been so cold. Bone-deep. Brain-core-deep frigid. It was almost like the jelly in her eyes had begun to physically freeze. Yet, something about the way the man moved seemed vaguely familiar. She shook her head and opened her eyes. "I just don't know. But someone helped me."

Annalise squirmed out of Zach's arms and struggled to exit the bed.

"Whoa! Where are you going?"

"To see him." She struggled to pull on the jeans she recognized as hers that someone had placed on the counter nearby.

Zach froze. "Kirk?"

"Yes. I have to, Zach. It's the only way to stop the nightmares."

"That doesn't make sense. His face... it's not him. It will make it worse."

She spun toward him, nearly falling back onto the bed as dizziness spiraled her brain and the jeans tangled her feet. "You saw him? Where?"

Zach's eyes darted toward the wall and then back. "In the shed."

"They must've dragged him in there afterwards. He was right out in the open. There were two of 'em. He was outnumbered. Never stood a chance." She shoved her foot into the other pants leg and yanked them to her waist. Dizziness didn't matter. "We have to get them, Zach. We have to make them pay."

He walked around the end of the bed and grabbed her shoulders.

She tried to shake him off, but he wouldn't budge.

"Look at me."

She refused to raise her gaze from the floor.

"Look at me, please, Lise."

It took every ounce of patience she possessed to look him in the eye and open her mind to what he prepared to say.

"It isn't our job to make them pay. It's our job to catch them, yes, but not to dole out their punishment."

She threw his hands from her shoulders. She didn't want to hear it. They'd killed Kirk right in front of her. What did Zach know about how that felt? What did he know about the horrendous bomb that seemed planted in the pit of her stomach? It threatened to blow the entire world to smithereens if she didn't get out of the hospital and start working. The buttons on her shirt would not go into the holes like they were supposed to. She growled.

"Here," Zach said gently. "Let me help."

Annalise's trembling hands dropped to her sides.

He delicately buttoned the shirt.

"I have to see him. I don't know why, but I need to."

Chapter Eleven

Annalise pulled in another deep breath. The cold doorhandle waited for her to twist and pull. A simple motion she'd done how many thousands of times?

"You sure this is a good idea?" Zach asked yet again.

She'd stopped counting how many after a dozen. Her stomach ignited in a mixture of hot flames and black terror. The door opened as easily as it always had, yet the weight of the situation pulled against her forward movement. She dragged her heavy feet across the tile.

Inside, Dr. Howard waited, a serene look upon his face. How many times had he done this? Given the family and friends of a corpse the chance to say goodbye. A chance to find closure in an impossible situation.

It wouldn't be closure for her, but rather fuel to feed the angry monster and drive it toward satisfying its craving for justice.

She stopped next to the sheet-covered form on the metal table. Zach placed his hand on her lower back. In slow motion, Dr. Howard pulled the sheet back to reveal Kirk's head and shoulders.

Bile sprang into her throat. She swallowed it back. His swollen and purple face, gashed and lacerated and split wide open in several places, didn't look at all like Kirk. Didn't even look human. One side of his skull no longer resembled anything close to a head. Her knees grew weaker.

Dr. Howard reached across the table and placed his hand on Annalise's shoulder. "Go home, Agent Baker. He's not here anymore."

Annalise nodded. She sniffled and swiped at tears she hadn't even known had fallen. Through cotton balls, she heard Zach thank Dr. Howard for staying after-hours for them. Robotically, she moved where his hand guided her.

Zach escorted her out and into his truck. The drive home flew by.

Millie greeted her as she swung the front door open, her tail wagging as happily as ever. Her sweet beagle nuzzled Annalise's hand. "Hey girl. I'm really sad." Annalise plopped onto the couch.

Millie jumped up next to her and placed her front paws and head in Annalise's lap.

"Thank you, sweet friend." Tears soaked the top of Millie's head.

In the kitchen, Zach banged dishes around. He presented her with a sandwich and fruit some moments later. "You need to try to eat."

"Not hungry."

"Doesn't matter. Eat."

She pushed past the nausea and managed a few bites. "What's next?"

"The funeral."

The food threatened to make a second appearance. "Tomorrow?"

He nodded and kissed the top of her head. "Listen, Annalise. I know the timing isn't superb." He coughed. "There's something I need to talk to you about."

A cold sweat broke out across her brow. Not more bad news. Not right now. She couldn't handle anything else.

He rose from the couch and knelt in front of her.

"Zach?" What was he doing? No, no, no. Not that...

"I love you. I don't want to go another minute without asking you to be mine. We've seen so much bad, Lise. Let's make some good together. Will you marry me?"

She felt the color drain from her face. How could he be thinking about marriage at a time like this? "Zach, I... don't know what to say."

"You love me. Say yes."

She popped to her feet and paced in front of the fireplace.

Millie whined at her from the couch.

"Zach, this is... I mean, of course, I love you. But now's not the time. Kirk's dead. We've got to focus on finding his killers. Once we catch them, we've got them because I—me, personally—can identify them. The case will be solid." She spun to face him. The look on his face cut her to the marrow.

He rose from the floor. "Think about it?"

She hadn't meant to hurt him. What did he expect? "I... yes, I'll think about it." Once she caught Kirk's murderers and could sleep one whole night without nightmares piercing her subconsciousness. Her shoulders stooped. "I'm sorry, Zach."

He moved toward the front door, placed his hand on the knob. "I'll pick you up at 8:30 in the morning. Okay?"

She nodded. Her body suddenly felt heavier than it ever had. "I love you."

"Yeah." He exited and shut the door behind him.

"I'm sorry," she whispered to the closed door.

Zach parked in Milt's driveway and cut the engine. Had he ever felt so low? He couldn't remember a time. For over half an hour, he sat in the driver's seat staring straight ahead, his mind racing but finding nothing steady to grasp onto.

A knock on the window beside his head made him jump and reach for his sidearm. He spun his head and found Milt smiling through the glass at him.

"You planning on sitting out here all night?"

Zach smiled despite himself. "Might."

"Come on in, young man. Tell me what's on your mind." Milt opened the truck door and motioned for him to exit.

Zach followed him into and through the house, exiting the rear onto a covered porch.

"Have a seat. I'll be right back."

Milt returned a moment later with two glasses of sweet tea and handed one to Zach. "All right, what's making that frown?"

"Annalise left the hospital against medical advice and is home."

Milt smiled. "I figured they'd not be able to hogtie her in much longer. Is she okay?"

"Seems to be."

"And?"

"I asked her to marry me. She said no."

Milt scratched his silver-whiskered chin. "What exactly did she say?"

"That she'd think about it."

"That's not no."

"Might as well be."

Milt tipped his amber-colored glass and took a long swig. He smacked his lips when he finished. "Don't you think you're being a little cynical? She didn't say no. Not to mention, with everything with Kirk... well, your timing could've been better."

Zach drew a deep breath in an attempt to calm the bubble of heat rising in his chest. "This whole thing has just made me realize how important Annalise is. How short life is. How tomorrow morning we're burying our friend, and I don't want to spend another night away from her."

"Did you say that?"

"Not exactly."

"You've known Annalise a long time. How does she usually handle grief, Zach?"

Zach tilted his head and thought. "Quietly. Alone."

"Injustice?"

Easy. "She fights like a honey badger trapped in a corner being poked with a sharp stick."

"So how about personal grief borne of extreme injustice?"

Zach sighed.

"Don't you think, that no matter how much she loves you, right now all she can think about is the fight ahead? About how much she must find Kirk's murderers or die herself?"

He nodded.

"Give her the time and support she needs. You know better than anyone that Annalise Raven Baker cannot be rushed, swayed, or forced."

"I know. I'm scared, Milt."

"Fear is a tool that the enemy uses to weaken us."

"It's highly effective."

Silence hovered over them until Milt lifted his glass and ice clinked against the side. "Want something to eat?"

"When have I ever said no to that?"

"I'll see what I can rustle up." Milt disappeared into the house.

Zach rocked and gazed out over the back yard. Milt's property ran down a gentle slope of manicured lawn into a dense old-growth forest. The bare trees under a clouded sky hid mysteries in its thick shadows. Zach shivered as the hairs on the back of his neck rose. Something wasn't right.

He inspected the shadows slowly, spending a couple seconds pausing on each one. There!

Someone waited behind a large white oak.

"Hey!"

The shape moved, melting into the forest.

Zach rose to his feet and bolted down the hill. Glass crashed behind him as his sweet tea fell to the porch. "Stop!"

He reached the edge of the trees and slipped into their cool shade. Pausing, he used a large trunk for cover and studied the landscape ahead. Something moved to his left. He drew his sidearm and slipped closer.

The form moved away, like magnets on same poles pushing against each other.

"Stop! Come out. I just want to talk!" How many cheesy detective stories started the death of one of the characters this way?

The person ran deeper into the woods. The way he moved…there was something about the way he moved. Zach stopped cold in his tracks.

Impossible.

Zach's heart pounded. It couldn't be. His father died. He had to be seeing things.

Footsteps approached behind him. He spun.

Milt wore a frown. "What's wrong?"

"Someone was watching us."

"Did you see who?"

A ghost. He shook his head. "No, never got a solid glimpse."

Milt glanced into the forest and back to Zach. "Well, whoever it was, they're gone now."

Zach swallowed. Nodded slowly. "Yeah. Gone now." Gone for months and months now. Permanently.

Chapter Twelve

The casket remained closed. Annalise breathed a sigh of relief. The people at the funeral home had no doubt made people appear "normal" after car wrecks, but they'd have to use a magic wand to recreate Kirk's normal face.

She stepped into the carpeted parlor room and noted the guests already filling the benches. Kirk's family waited at the front of the long line.

Her knees grew weak. "I can't—"

Zach placed his hand on her back. "You can. You will because you have to. It's the right thing to do, and my Lise always does the right thing."

If only Zach knew what thoughts had occupied her entire lonely night. In fact, she'd been too afraid to sleep. She and Millie had watched TV, and she had paced a track in her living room floor, and she had watched the sunrise grow rosy in a frosty morning air.

But the thoughts had never stopped swirling. They swam at the fringes even now. The men who had done this had to pay. She clenched her fists, digging her nails into her palms, counted to ten, and released them.

Where did Buchanan run? He had no other property in his name, not according to their previous searches. He had to know someone. Had to have more connections.

She guffawed. Connections that were strong enough to get him released from prison when he clearly was guilty.

Maybe Kirk knew those details and that's why those men had beaten...

Tears climbed into her eyes. She couldn't let them fall. Kirk's wife deserved those tears. His daughter deserved those tears. She had no right to cry over Kirk when she watched him die and did nothing to stop it.

The line inched forward.

Kirk's little girl burst through the rear door and ran to the front. She wrapped her arms around her mommy's waist and smiled up at her. From where she and Zach stood, Annalise couldn't hear the girl's words. But her curly, blonde-haired head bobbed a few times, and then she was off, racing out the door a different direction.

Grief sucker punched her in the gut. She nearly doubled over with the pain. Lydia would grow up without a father. Would never remember the friend and strong man Annalise had come to love as a valued member of her circle. Why had God taken him so soon? What possible good could come of his death?

Before she was ready, it was her turn to shake Ms. Johnson's hand. The empty look in Grace's eyes sent a chill rocketing down Annalise's spine.

What could she say? Nothing would help. She squeezed Grace's hand, trying to pass some of her strength to the grieving widow.

Grace weakened and then threw her arms around Annalise's neck. "Find them, Agent Baker. They can't get away with doing this to a good man."

Concrete solidified in Annalise's gut. The tears tamped down, replaced with fire. She nodded. "I promise."

Grace released her.

Annalise moved robotically through the room to her seat.

Zach slid in beside her and put his arm around her shoulders. "You okay?"

"No."

The crowd pressing around Kirk's grave spilled over onto the gravel road winding through the cemetery. What would this black-clad group look like from above? Zach closed his eyes and imagined an aerial shot of the scene. He didn't know why, but it brought him comfort.

All these people loved Kirk in some way. If even a small amount of the good man they'd known existed in each of these people, Kirk would never be forgotten. His presence in the world would never completely disappear.

Annalise squeezed his hand. His eyes flew open.

"Look," she whispered.

On the fence line several hundred yards to the far side, three men in black suits waited. Standing out mostly because of their lack of conspicuousness. Zach glared at their sunglass-hidden faces and frowned. They didn't belong here.

They placed the folded flag in Grace's hands. A single tear slid down the widow's pale cheek. As the crowd dispersed, the men approached.

Zach whispered, "Be right back."

Annalise nodded.

Milt stepped out and headed the same direction. Zach nodded toward him, a heavy weight settling in the pit of his stomach. The men stopped under a shady tree, arms crossed over their chests. Suited triplets with stony faces. He and Milt reached them at the same time.

"Can we help you gentleman with something?" Zach asked.

The one on the left spoke up. "Agents Halsley, Parker, and Burchfield. We need to speak with Annalise Baker."

"Special Agent Baker," Milt said, emphasizing the special agent, "is grieving a dear friend and mentor. You can come back later."

"It won't wait till later," the same agent said.

"I'm her partner. Tell me whatever you'd tell her." Zach glanced at Annalise, who now stood alone at Kirk's casket. He could tell by the way her shoulders shook just how hard she sobbed. "Tell me."

The men exchanged quick glances, then the same one spoke. "Buchanan is off-limits. Period. Leave him alone."

Blood rushed to Zach's head. If it hadn't been for Milt's steadying hand on his shoulder, he would've popped the man in the nose. "You realize what they've done?"

"We're aware of the situation," agent number two said.

"Then you understand the grave—" Zach pointed to Annalise bawling over the coffin "—consequences of their actions."

The men's gazes returned to cement.

Zach strained against Milt's hands, now both grasping at him, one on his chest and the other on his elbow. "You'll have to arrest me and throw me in the deepest pits of Azkaban to stop us from finding Kirk's murderers."

"We have powers you cannot imagine," the third agent said.

Zach gritted his teeth. Paused. Blew out a breath. "We have vengeance you've never dreamed of. Stay out of our way."

He shook Milt's hand off and strode back to Annalise's side. The conversation tagged along, distance not dissolving the anger one tiny bit.

"What's wrong?"

"I—I don't want to tell you."

She swiped her sleeve across her damp cheeks. "What is it?"

"Those men were just… um… giving me an update. They've lost Buchanan." The lie didn't set well in his mouth or his heart.

"Doesn't matter. We'll find him."

He had no doubt that Annalise would follow through with that promise. But at what consequence?

Chapter Thirteen

Annalise slung her backpack over her shoulders and cinched the straps tight. "Ready?"

Zach nodded.

"No time to waste." She strode into the forest where she and Kirk had entered only a few short days before. He hadn't come back. She had, a million times heavier under the weight of his death.

An hour and a half later, they emerged to Buchanan's small clearing. She gave the shed a wide berth, cut the DO NOT CROSS tape, and entered his cabin. If there was a clue here, she'd find it.

The investigation team had taken nearly everything from his cabin. Annalise sighed. Why was she here? All the evidence already lived in some FBI storehouse somewhere, and she'd never see it.

The corner of the living room that appeared to have once housed a computer on the desk now sat empty. The filing cabinet that presumably once held important documents also gave no treasures when she slid the drawers open. Buchanan's sleeping area had been thoroughly combed. Even most of his clothes had been taken from the closet.

Annalise tapped the walls and the floor. A man like Buchanan would have places to hide his most important secrets.

"Annalise, come here!"

Zach's excitement floated in through the front door. He disappeared before she could ask anything else. She raced to follow him down the cellar stairs and stopped cold as she reached the bottom. The last time she'd entered this space, she'd rescued a terrified hurt boy whose family she now called friends. Her heart sped up. She never thought in a million years she'd have to be back in this cold, dank space.

"Come here." Zach motioned from the corner situated under the kitchen above. "Look at this."

A section of blocks appeared different, less mud-stained, than the others. He shined a light into a crack. She peered inside. "No way." Brass hinges reflected the flashlight glow. "Open it."

"How?"

Annalise checked for a handle or button or something. "What do you suppose they use?"

"I dunno. Be right back."

Zach returned a few minutes later with a crowbar and a sheepish grin. "Found it in the shed."

She shrugged. "Go for it."

He slid the bar into the crack and pried. The blocks cracked. Something popped within, and Zach nearly toppled over. She stuck her fingers in the crack and wiggled. The block fell free. On the other side, a dark chamber, about five feet square, held a few dozen cardboard boxes.

"Do it again." She smiled.

Zach pulled the next three or four blocks free.

She stepped into the room. "These hold answers, Zach. I just know it. Can you please help me carry them upstairs?"

"Of course."

It took them each six trips to bring all of them to the kitchen table, some stacked two tall. Annalise's mind whirred. She sucked in a cleansing breath and tried to slow down. She couldn't hurry. She'd miss something. And that was unacceptable.

She lifted the lid to find a stack of notebooks. She flipped open the first one. In the upper right-hand corner, the date of 09/15/1997 had been sketched in blue pen and messy handwriting. Neat columns and rows with records of moonshine sales filled the pages. Initials that she presumed represented clients, dates, prices, vat numbers. She looked at the stacks of boxes. If all these only held record books for his business, then maybe they weren't so useful after all. She spread the boxes out and flipped all the lids off. Every single one held notebooks upon notebooks upon notebooks.

"Help me open them all up to the first page."

She and Zach worked to put the boxes in chronological order. Hours passed in relative quiet, with only the sound of the pages rustling filling the cabin.

In the middle of a stack of notebooks in box eleven, Annalise finally found something different. "Zach, look at this."

"What is it?"

"Property ledgers. I think."

"That Buchanan owns?"

"I'm not sure. Possibly."

Zach leaned back against the wall. "But that doesn't make sense, does it? If Buchanan had a bunch of land holdings out there somewhere, wouldn't we have found them on our search last year?"

Annalise shrugged. "All of this is off the books. Why wouldn't property be too?"

"Good point."

"Do you think they went to one of these places?"

"It would make sense. A man like Buchanan would've had backups. We closed down his main still, but it would be foolish of us to assume we stopped his business completely."

"Don't you think the feds would know? I mean, I've been thinking. Maybe Buchanan didn't know anything. Maybe they've put him back into the position so they can catch bigger fish."

"A mole?"

"Yeah.

"It's crossed my mind too. Do you really think it's that simple?"

"Could be. We know the Moonshine Mafia and your dad's drug cartel are in the same general locale now. Maybe Buchanan is supposed to infiltrate the cartel?" She glanced at Zach's face. His glossy eyes and frown reminded her she'd touched a nerve. She placed her hand on his forearm. "Sorry. I didn't mean to—"

He shook his head. "It's fine. My father was what he was. Nothing I can do about it now."

Her stomach knotted. His words didn't match his feelings. She knew him too well to miss when he lied.

She began riffling through pages again, photographing the pages of asset inventory. At some point, they'd have to bring four-wheelers out and get these boxes. Which meant telling Kirk she'd gone behind his back again…

Kirk.

She'd never have to worry about reporting to him again. Her breathing became shallow. Tears blurred her vision. How many times in the coming weeks and months would she forget?

Would she have to reawaken to the realization he'd been brutally beaten and murdered right in front of her?

"Lise? What's wrong?"

"I… I forgot."

Zach drew her into his arms and held her while she sobbed.

Their once-peace-inducing headquarters now filled Zach with a gray heaviness as he entered the front door. Avoiding looking toward Kirk's open door, Zach beelined straight into his and set his backpack on the desk. It'd been fun hiking out with two dozen notebooks weighing it down even more than normal. Not.

As soon as his bottom touched his chair, the phone rang. Annalise's muffled voice sounded from her office answering the call. He sighed. Good. He wasn't in the mood to deal with anyone right now.

Annalise's voice stopped echoing through the empty hallway. Instead, her footsteps approached. She hovered silently in the doorway until Zach looked up. Her pale face shouted what she couldn't seem to get out of her open mouth.

He rose to his feet. "Lise, what is it?"

"Brit's dead."

"Who?"

"Kirk's source. I—I talked to her about Buchanan. She warned me away, and now she's dead."

He rounded the desk and put his hands on her shoulders. His heart ached for her. "It's not your fault."

"Everyone around me is dying."

"Not me." He smiled, but his attempted joke fell flat.

A tear slid down her cheek. She swiped it away with an angry hand. "How do I even have tears left?" She pulled free from his hands. "They found her body on the riverbank."

"Cause of death?"

"Too soon to tell, but there's a bullet wound. They want us to join them."

"Are you ready for that?"

"No." She shrugged. "We don't really have a choice. The orders are coming from main office."

The bigwigs. "I've haven't talked to anyone at main since the team was formed and turned over to Kirk. Have you?" Not their main office anyway. The feds didn't count, did they?

She shook her head. "Who do you think they'll get to replace him?"

"I don't know that they'll find anyone like Kirk." He clamped his lips together to keep them from trembling. Maybe it was time to tell her about the FBI agent's threat. Was Brit dead because she'd refused to walk away? He cleared his throat. "Guess we need to call Oliver Tobias, eh?"

"I'll just shoot him a text." She winced. "Sorry. Poor choice of words."

Zach yawned, suddenly hyperaware of the fact that he hadn't really slept more than a couple hours in days. "Think he's back from returning the truck to Piston already? And picking mine up?"

"Hopefully. He can take lead on this one."

"Good idea."

Annalise started through his door, then swung around suddenly. "Ever feel like everything is spinning around you really fast and you're reaching out and grabbing for pieces but nothing will stick and your hands hurt and you're tired and you're numb and yet you have to just keep reaching and sprinting for some finish line that's really far away?" She huffed. "And it's dark."

Zach raised his left eyebrow. "Can't say that I have."

"Great." She crossed her arms and stomped down the hallway.

Awesome. He'd managed to stick his foot in his mouth again. Speaking of which, was she ever going to answer his question? His life-altering, momentous question. It wasn't like he'd asked what she wanted for dinner. He'd asked her to marry him, and he still had no answer.

Milt's voice niggled the back of his mind. *Your timing's a bit off, son.* That's what

Annalise's father had said. It'd even been what he'd said in his rushed and not-romantic-at-all proposal. He groaned. The most beautiful and important woman in the world deserved more than what he'd given her in that moment. No wonder she didn't feel like answering.

He hurried to her office, rounding the corner already talking. "Annalise, I'm sorry—"

Annalise sat in her chair, head on her desk, her shoulders heaving in gut-wrenching sobs.

He rushed to her side, pried her from her desk, and redirected her head to his shoulder. She didn't fight. She barely even felt like she was anything but a puddle of pudding in his arms. "Shhh, it's okay, love. It's going to be okay." He stroked her hair until she calmed.

"I'm so angry, Zach. So, so angry. I wasn't even this mad during the divorce."

His skin crawled at the mention of her ex-husband. That was one person he could definitely spend the rest of his life happily without.

Chapter Fourteen

Annalise squatted next to Brit's bluish-tinted, swollen body and bit back the bile rising in her throat. After a cursory glance, she decided that the victim's body held no immediate clues and nodded to Dr. Howard. "Take her in."

"Yes, ma'am." He patted Annalise's shoulder before beginning the process of transferring Brit's corpse to the stretcher.

Nearby, Zach stared across Little Pigeon River, a blank expression on his face. She approached. "Care to share what's on your mind?"

He didn't turn toward her. "No."

Ouch. She drew a calming breath, then hooked her arm around his. His hand remained buried in his pocket. "What do we do now?"

He shrugged.

As they stood gazing across the icy waters, the distance between them grew wider. She'd meant what do they do about the case, but she knew he'd taken it to mean what were they supposed to do about their relationship. Did she want to marry Zach?

She dug around the emotions tied to Kirk and Buchanan and Brit, sorting them into separate piles and attempting to find the container that held hers and Zach's love. It was still there, but getting to it felt like looking for a diamond buried in a landfill.

"I love you, Zach." Her words felt hollow, though she knew them to be true.

"I love you too, Annalise."

She pulled her arm free and spun him to face her. "We'll figure *everything* out once we catch Buchanan. Okay?"

He nodded.

She glanced over his shoulder at movement in the parking lot. Her heart stopped beating.

"Annalise? What's wrong?"

He spun to look where her gaze stuck.

She placed her hand on his back, unable to speak. His muscles tensed under her touch.

"It can't be." He growled and then took several rapid steps forward.

The man moved. If it wasn't Henry Leebow in the flesh, it was him in specter. Her heart snapped to life. "Is that…"

Henry nodded toward them, then slipped inside a black compact car.

"He means for us to follow," Annalise whispered.

They ran to Zach's truck, hopped in, and flew to the parking lot's exit to catch up.

"Which way?" Zach said.

She scanned the street both directions. "There!"

Zach whipped the truck toward the right and accelerated. Her heart hammered her lungs as they hugged the car's bumper for a few miles around winding roads, until it abruptly pulled into a diner situated in an old railcar.

Glued to the seat, she watched Henry stroll into the restaurant without a single look their way. This was a movie. It had to be.

Zach opening his door spurred her to action. She scurried to catch up. He flung the door open and stalked into the small dining area, Annalise on his heels. Zach stopped. She slammed into his back, then peered over his shoulder.

His breathing sped up.

Sure enough, Henry Leebow, in the flesh, alive and seemingly well, sat in the booth in the farthest corner.

Henry met Zach's glare. His breath stuck in his chest. He'd seen him recently, from a distance. He'd been watching over them both. But here, this close, preparing himself to speak to the boy that had made him a father, it felt different.

In slow motion, they approached and slid into the booth, Annalise on the inside. Zach sat like a cat on a fencepost. Ready to spring into action and speed away at the slightest ruffle of his fur.

"Annalise, it's good to see you alive and well." He spun the coffee cup in front of him slowly. Then he slid a flash drive across the table.

Zach hissed out a long breath.

Annalise opened her mouth, closed it, then finally spoke. "I'd like to say the same thing about you, but I'm not sure how to feel."

He pressed his lips together in a tight smile. "I deserved that. We have a lot to discuss."

"Do we?" Zach snapped. "It isn't exactly your strong suit. Communication and all."

"I deserved that too."

Zach turned to glare out the window.

The barn cat had morphed into a mountain lion ready to tear him limb from limb. "Zach, listen. I know this is hard to believe, after everything, but I did what I had to do to protect everyone involved."

"I've heard that before."

"That's because it's the truth, son."

Red flushed Zach's neck and cheeks. Henry leaned back into the plush bench and sighed.

"We'll have to cover all this later." He tapped the flash drive.

"What's this?" Annalise crossed her arms over her chest.

"Proof."

"Of what?"

"That the Moonshine Mafia murdered the Zucker kid," Henry said. "It's a recording. Of the men talking."

"How?"

"Not important. But, what is important." Henry paused. "I know where Buchanan is."

Her arms fell to the tabletop. Her face paled.

Zach sat like a statue.

"This is all going to make sense. I promise. The most important thing is to get him now, while we still can."

"How do you propose we do that?" Annalise asked.

"He's holed up in another one of his properties. A cave house."

"Seriously?" she said.

"Seriously. It's virtually impenetrable." He took a swig of coffee. "And your ME is going to discover that Brit was killed with a .45 that matches another murder."

"Who?" Zach asked without turning his head.

"Remember the guy that washed up in the rainstorm when Buchanan had the Moss boy captured?"

They both nodded.

"But that gun is in evidence from Buchanan's murder and kidnapping investigation," Annalise said.

"Not anymore. Buchanan has it."

Finally, Zach turned to face him. "How?"

Henry leaned in and lowered his voice. "I gave it to him."

Zach imagined himself flying over the table at his father. Gripping his neck and squeezing until his father's eyes bulged. Then the blistering energy scalding his veins would have an outlet.

Instead, he bit his tongue until he tasted the coppery zing of blood.

"You what?" Annalise hissed.

"Buchanan framed me. I never led the gang, drugs or moonshine or any kind. I was deep under cover, but I never—never—"

At this second never, Zach could feel his father's gaze burning a hole through his head. He didn't cave to the pressure and, instead, continued to laser beam the glass window next to their booth.

"Joined them or dropped my defenses. There came a point where I knew exactly how it looked and exactly what was going to happen."

"When was that?"

Zach could have applauded Annalise's oozing sarcasm. If he felt like any of his body could actually move.

"I began to make plans to extricate myself from the situation. But Buchanan and the cartel did a bang-up job of making me look guilty. No one I normally count on could be trusted. So I faked my death."

"How is that even possible? You couldn't have achieved that solo." Annalise slammed her back into the bench seat and crossed her arms. "I don't buy it."

"Do you believe in ghosts?" Henry grinned, though it didn't reach his eyes.

"No," Zach ground out through clenched teeth. "I don't believe in ghosts. And I don't believe a word you're spilling out of your lying, filthy mouth either." His entire body shook as he pushed himself free of the table and stormed out the door. Annalise followed him. At the truck, he laid his arms over the edge of the bed and hung his head between them.

The shallow breaths he gasped for didn't seem to be reaching any of his body.

Annalise rubbed his back in small circles.

He shook her off. "I could kill him."

"I already did." Annalise chuckled.

"That's not funny." But it sort of was in a really not funny, horrible, deceptive, manipulative way. He straightened and drew her into his arms. "How do I handle this one, Lise?"

"I have no idea."

Having her in his arms calmed him enough to be able to see straight, at least. He released her. They leaned against the truck next to each other. "Do you believe him?"

"Oddly enough, yes," she replied.

"Me too." The story made so little sense that it made sense. Zach's heart lifted a smidgen higher. If his father told the truth now, it meant he wasn't a villain back then. Wasn't the lying crooked agent everyone had said. It certainly didn't make up for Henry abandoning him and his mom, but, somehow, it helped something.

"So, what now?" Annalise said.

"We go get Buchanan."

Chapter Fifteen

Zach pulled into Annalise's driveway and put the truck in PARK. Annalise sighed. A quick shower and change of clothes, then Henry and Oliver Tobias would be here for a meeting to formulate their plan. She glanced at Zach's profile. Tense jaw muscles told her he still mulled everything over.

Millie trotted around the corner of the house toward them. Weird. Annalise never left Millie out alone. She barely even remembered the last time she'd been home. The emotional rollercoaster blurred everything that had happened in the last few days.

"Did your mom come walk Millie for me?" Annalise wrinkled her brows together.

"Not that I know of."

They exited the truck, and Annalise squatted to scratch Millie's ears. "How'd you get out, ole girl?"

Millie's tail wagged.

Annalise rose and stepped toward the front walk.

Millie blocked her forward progress by placing her furry body between Annalise and the steps.

"Move, girl."

Millie whined.

Annalise maneuvered around her and plodded up the staircase.

Millie's toenails sounded like rabbits scratching to escape a cardboard box as she raced up the steps, again planting herself between Annalise and the front door.

She nearly tripped. "Millie, what on earth? Are you that mad at me? I'm sorry if I forgot to put you up this morning." She patted her soft ears. "I know you missed the couch."

Zach hollered from where he still stood next to the truck, "What's wrong with her?"

She half-turned toward him. "I don't know. She never does this."

"Do you think…"

So many thoughts ran amok, Annalise didn't know on which to focus.

Zach bounded up the steps and flew past her and Millie.

"What? Zach! What is it?"

At the top of the steps, he pulled his gun and pressed his back to the house. He met her glance.

Was someone inside? Her heart thrummed as she grabbed Millie's collar and dragged her to the truck. Millie reluctantly jumped into the passenger seat, and Annalise gently closed the door. She padded up the steps and joined Zach. Nodded once. He swung the front door open and disappeared inside. She knew he'd go left, so when she followed, she cleared right.

Nothing appeared out of place. They worked in tandem, silently, to clear the main areas of the house, making their way toward the back hallway. She stopped outside her closed bedroom door. Closed? The morning blurred in her memory, but she didn't remember closing the door.

She drew a steadying breath and turned the handle slowly. She had to push harder on the door than normally, and when it swung open, something clicked. "What was that?" she hissed toward Zach.

His eyes grew wide, and his face drained of all color. He grabbed her wrist and dragged her toward the living room. "Run!"

As they emerged from the hallway, something shoved her violently forward. She crashed into Zach's back, and they both fell to the floor. Seconds later, the blast sound reached her ears.

The entire world's sounds turned into a piercing ring. She clapped her hands to her ears. Heat rolled over her. She was vaguely aware of

Zach's body under her, wriggling to get free. Her own body failed to respond to her commands.

When he freed himself, she rolled over and stared down the hallway toward her splintered wall and bedroom door. A ball of fire tumbled out of the opening, licking the wood floor as it sped her direction. She reached for Zach, tugging hard at his ankles. He crashed to the floor just as the boiling waves of flame tumbled over them. The heat stung her face. Her hair crackled, but the whoosh passed over them and extinguished in the empty space.

"Are you okay?" she hollered above the growing rage of the fire consuming the back half of her home.

"I think so! Come on!" He grabbed her hand and pulled her to her feet.

They sprinted for the front door.

Halfway there, Henry ran through the opening. He grabbed ahold of Zach's shoulders and dragged him out the door.

Oliver Tobias entered and snagged Annalise's arm. "What happened?" he yelled as they emerged into fresh air.

"I… don't… know." Annalise bent double and coughed until she saw stars. "Where's Zach?"

"He's with some older guy, but he seems fine."

Annalise glanced toward Zach and Henry. Millie stood at their feet barking frantically.

Neither of the men seemed to notice. Annalise coughed again, gulping oxygen into her starved lungs afterward. "There was a bomb. In my bedroom."

Oliver Tobias's face flushed red. "What?"

"You heard me right."

"I'll be right back."

The heat singed his right side as he ducked around to the back of Annalise's once-beautiful cabin. A pang seized him. Even if the fire department showed up right this second, her house was a total loss.

He circled to the rear and climbed the incline. Looking down at her house from this angle, he could see straight through most of the rear windows, into the bedrooms, and had a partial visual of the parking area. This is how he would've approached the house.

The thick grove of pine trees provided little room for footprints with years' worth of brown needles matting the ground. A fleck of white poked out between some leaves, and he bent to retrieve it. He wrapped the leaf around it and lifted a cigarette butt. No doubt, not Annalise's or Zach's.

Even from this distance, the heat radiated from the intensity of the blaze. Sirens echoed from somewhere far away. He imagined the heavy trucks scaling the switchback road, lugging their water bellies behind a groaning engine. The house cracked under the weight of the fire's scarlet and orange fingers. Something fell, sending a gasp of sparks skyward. Oddly beautiful. He shook himself from the entrancement and made his way back to Annalise and Zach.

She now knelt, with Millie hugged to her chest, and watched with an ash-streaked face as her home melted. The flames reflected in her liquid eyes so that Oliver Tobias didn't have to turn to see what happened behind him. Anger radiated from her, shooting like laser beams from her pupils.

He knew that feeling. *Lord, help us.*

Zach's heart broke along with the beams dying inside Annalise's cabin.

The fire trucks arrived and lurched to a stop. The men inside sprinted out, slinging gear on as they ran. Pulling hoses. Shouting commands.

It didn't matter. The wouldn't be able to save the house. *Thank you, Lord, that we are okay and that Millie was outside.* Annalise would've been distraught if Millie had been injured or killed.

He made his way to her side. The look in her eye—that of a motherless fawn, wide, dark orbs of emotion—made him tremble. When had he ever seen his sweet Annalise with that much intensity? That much anger? He looked away. Despite the heat from the fire, a chill ran through him.

"We need to get moving," Henry whispered over his shoulder.

Zach resisted the urge to elbow his father in the stomach and then backhand him in the nose and then stomp on him as he lay gasping for breath.

He snorted. Annalise's and his volatility made for highly professional special agents at the moment.

Annalise seemed to not have heard Henry, so Zach bent to her, gently laid his hand on her back, and spoke, "Ready?"

She spun eyes toward him that burned hotter than the blaze. "I'll ride with Oliver Tobias. We'll follow you and Henry."

Zach's gut churned. Great. Alone time with dear old dad.

He chewed on his bottom lip and stared out the window for the first several miles. At six miles, his leg began to bounce. He'd counted sixty-seven cars. At twenty, the words pressed against his tongue. At twenty-one, he could hold them back no longer.

"Why didn't you *tell* me?" He turned to stare at his father's profile. "Why didn't you say something—anything—that would've made all of this better? Easier?"

If Henry was surprised, it didn't show. "It was too dangerous."

"Oh, bologna. Too dangerous for who? You? Too hard for you to tell the truth for once in your life."

That's not fair, son.

Lord? Are you serious? Not fair in what world?

When Henry didn't respond, Zach continued. "I was in a good place with you."

Henry chuckled. "You thought I was dead."

"Exactly."

"Wow. That one stung, son. Congratulations."

"Congratulations?" He said it more to himself than to Henry. What had he been trying to accomplish? *Hurting him. I want him to hurt the way I do. Have wanted that for years.* "People—lots of people—are dead because of you."

Henry slammed on the brakes, jerked to the side of the interstate. His knuckles on the steering wheel turned white. His breath came in ragged huffs. "You think I don't know that? Think I don't struggle with that every night when I close my eyes?"

"You had a family to raise! You left mom. You left me!" Tears gathered in Zach's eyes. He shoved them back.

His father's chin fell to his chest. "What was I supposed to do, son? I did my job really well, and somehow I still took the fall for things that shouldn't have been my burden to bear."

Chinks of armor started to crumble from Zach's heart. He attempted catch them and re-lay the bricks that kept him safe from his father reaching him. "I needed you."

"I'm here now." Henry raised his gaze to Zach's.

Zach couldn't meet it. It wasn't enough, the here now. Far too little, far too late.

Chapter Sixteen

Annalise's clothes smelled like smoke. Millie's fur too. Sitting on the side of the highway in Oliver Tobias's truck, she stroked Millie's neck absentmindedly. The animated forms of the men in front of them told her exactly what she'd known was coming. Maybe they could find common ground? Or at least distance themselves from the battle ground.

Henry and Zach's "discussion" lasted only a few minutes, and then Henry whipped the vehicle back into traffic and accelerated.

In her haze, she'd not even thought to ask where they were headed.

"You okay?" Oliver Tobias asked quietly.

She tilted her head for a few moments. "Not really sure."

"That's understandable."

"Thanks."

"I'm sorry about your home."

"Me too." A new thought slammed into her. Where was she going to stay? How it hadn't occurred to her yet, she didn't understand. But the force of it certainly stole what tiny shred of peace she had left. Maybe Zach's mom? They'd dropped Millie off with her already. What was one more stray?

Oliver Tobias glanced into the rearview mirror. "Oh."

"What?" Annalise spun to check behind them. Two black SUVs with tinted windows flew onto their bumper. The lead Cadillac whipped around them, dashed in front of Henry and Zach, and slammed on their brakes.

Annalise lurched toward the dash as Oliver Tobias crushed the brake pedal. Her seatbelt caught. Pain shot through her collarbone and into her shoulder. What in the world? A second later Oliver Tobias's truck crashed into Henry's bumper. It always surprised her just how loud metal crunching could be.

Her body flung toward the center console, then back toward the door. Her head bounced off the window, adding to the pain already searing her arm and shoulder. Glass crunched and shattered. Chunks of cascading sparkles flew through the cab.

It ended in mere moments, and Annalise sat rigidly, running a mental check of her body parts. Arms, hurting but not broken. Legs, surprisingly fine. Head, throbbing. Concussion? Neck, screaming.

"Oliver Tobias? You okay?" she asked without turning her head. The idea of moving those neck muscles did not appeal to her.

"Mmm-hmmm." He coughed. "Barely."

Zach! She pulled the door handle. Bent metal screeched and yielded unwillingly to her shoving. She stumbled from the truck and searched their surroundings for Henry's vehicle. Oliver Tobias's truck had come to rest against a sapling no bigger than her wrist. How had that tiny thing stopped a half-ton pickup?

Through the dingey gray trunks, she spied a flash of color. Something tickled her forehead. She reached to swipe it and found blood coating her fingers. Great.

She crashed through the underbrush, stumbling over a downed tree, and reached Henry's SUV. Steam hissed out around the edges of the crumpled hood. "Zach!"

Neither man appeared to be in the vehicle.

Where had they gone? She pressed her eyes closed and listened through the swirling stabs of red and pink knives in her brain. Shouting to her left drew her attention. She made her way toward it.

As she emerged from the forest, she spotted Zach and Henry on the highway, guns drawn. Each of them aimed for a stopped black SUV with a crinkled rear bumper and smoking tires.

"Get out of the vehicle!" Zach shouted, his face red.

The driver's side and passenger doors swung open simultaneously. Two men in dark jeans and t-shirts exited with their hands raised. Both of them wore smiles.

Interesting…

Oliver Tobias emerged behind her. "Think we should help?"

Help? "Yeah, that would be a good idea."

He withdrew his weapon and approached the vehicle. Annalise didn't move. Dizziness threatened to collapse her legs. Nausea rose. Annalise sank to the ground and grabbed her temples. Pressing them, hard, made the world stop violently spinning.

She could no longer hear what the men said. Soon, though, the second SUV returned, and the men got into the back seat and sped away.

Zach turned toward her. His mouth opened, then closed. He sprinted to her and knelt. "You're bleeding."

She knew that already.

"We need to get you to the hospital."

She pushed his hands away. "I'm fine." She wasn't. "Who was that? Why did you let them go?"

Zach's heart sank. Time to come clean. "Let's get to the hospital."

"How, Zach?"

Good question. Both vehicles were out of commission. A siren sounded in the distance. He glanced around. Several cars had stopped. One of the onlookers must've called 9-1-1. He sank to the grass beside her. "Feds."

"What?"

"The men. They're FBI."

"Oh."

"At Kirk's funeral, did you see me talking to the suited men under the tree?"

"Yeah. I assumed they were associates of Kirk's or something."

"They weren't. They warned us off the case." His heart pounded as he waited for her response.

"I understand why you didn't tell me."

He opened his mouth to argue. Wait. What?

"I'm not going in that ambulance. Call Milt." She rose, tottered, and started to walk away.

"Annalise, stop." He grabbed her shoulders and spun her to face him. A tear escaped each beautiful, hazel eye. "Where are you going?"

She frowned. "To the rock house. Wherever that is." She pointed to Henry, who waited in the shadows nearby.

"Let the medics bandage you up, at least."

"Fine. Then we go. This ends today."

Zach knew Annalise's determination well. But this—this reached a whole new level.

The ambulance arrived, followed by a fire truck and a police officer. Zach spun to find his father. Henry had melted into the forest, like a stealthy deer, and vanished.

The medics jogged to where he and Annalise stood. The female addressed Annalise, "Ma'am, you need to sit down and stop moving. Does anything hurt?"

"Well, the gash on my forehead doesn't feel so hot."

The medic's nostrils flared, Zach bit back a chuckle.

The male medic spoke to him. "Sir, how about you? What happened here?"

Zach swallowed. "Ran off the road." He pointed behind them. "SUV's up against a tree back yonder. We're okay."

He scanned the tree line. Oliver Tobias, too, had disappeared.

"We need to transport you both to the hospital. Check for head trauma," the female medic said while attempting to slip a C-collar around Annalise's neck.

Annalise pushed her away. "No thanks."

"I really must insist, ma'am."

"I said, no. Thanks. I'm fine." She turned to face him, grabbing his elbow and pulling him away from the medic team. "Did you get ahold of Milt?"

"He texted. He's on his way."

"How long?"

Zach glanced toward the highway. "There he is now."

Milt pulled to the shoulder in front of the ambulance.

The medics watched them, mouths agape, as they speed-walked to Milt's truck and climbed into the cab.

Zach turned in time to see a police officer running their direction. "Wait!"

Milt pulled into the free lane ahead. "You two okay? What happened?"

Zach waited a moment for Annalise to answer, but when she didn't he spoke. "FBI ran us off the road. The guys from the funeral."

"No way."

"How'd you end up bein' so close, Milt?"

"Got a text with an address to meet."

Annalise still stared straight ahead, glassy-eyed.

"So you just decided you'd take off and see what or who was on the other end?

"Ain't the first time, young man."

"It's Henry."

Milt's foot slipped off the gas pedal. "Can't be."

Zach nodded. "Sure as I live and breathe."

"I knew it!" Milt depressed the pedal again.

"We need to pull over as soon as we're out of sight."

At the next bend, Milt swung back to the shoulder and stopped. "What are we waitin' for exactly?"

Zach grinned. "You'll see." He scanned the forest. Nothing moved. Yet. "You knew what, Milt?"

"That your old man wasn't dead."

"How?"

"No way he did the things they say he did."

"What makes you so sure?"

"You forget I knew him a long time ago, young man. A long time ago."

Annalise finally spoke, "There." She raised a steady finger and pointed at an angle to their right. Sure enough, Oliver Tobias and Henry ducked under a low branch and emerged. They checked both directions and sprinted to the truck. Each leaped over the bed sides and landed with a barely perceptible thunk. Oliver Tobias knocked on the window as Henry and he slid out of sight below the edges.

Milt pulled out.

"Henry's the only one who knows where we're going," Zach mumbled.

Milt whipped out his phone and showed him the last text from a blocked number. "I assume this is our destination."

Zach programmed it into his Google Maps app, and twenty minutes later they wound down a narrow gravel road beneath a canopy of ink-lined tree branches.

Steep mountains pressed upon them. Blue sky became visible only in sporadic bursts. Sunlight never reached the ground. Zach shivered. Whatever lay ahead would be almost as difficult as what lay behind him. Literally.

Chapter Seventeen

Several miles down the gravel road, Henry tapped on the rear glass. A flare of red and orange emotion shot through Annalise's chest. Buchanan hid somewhere nearby. Kirk's killers most likely with him.

Milt stopped the truck and rolled down the window.

"See the pull-off up there?" Henry asked, leaning over the roof.

"Barely," Milt answered.

"Exactly. We walk from here." Henry hopped out of the bed on the driver's side.

Oliver Tobias jumped to the gravel on the passenger side. Zach opened the door, and she and he slid out. Milt parked the truck, and Henry stood several thickly leaved rhododendron cuts behind it.

He reached into the bed and withdrew a duffle bag Annalise hadn't noticed till this moment.

From it, he dispensed four AR-15s with extra ammunition magazines for each of them. Annalise's heart began to speed up. What were they walking into?

Henry patted her shoulder. "Don't know what to expect exactly. Better to be prepared."

She nodded. "The feds know about this place?"

"I suspect they do."

She grimaced. "They on their way then?"

"Most likely."

"We'd better work quickly then, eh?"

Henry nodded. "I need Buchanan alive to clear my name."

Annalise winced.

"You understand?"

She did. But she didn't like it. If ever a man deserved to die at the other end of a gun, it was Buchanan.

Not your job.

Annalise sucked in a breath. But it was her job, wasn't it? If the jails couldn't hold him and the feds could just set him free at any moment, it was her job to take him out. To end his reign of evil.

Vengeance is mine, sayeth the Lord.

I don't understand what You want me to do.

Justice. Not vengeance, child.

There is no justice! Buchanan had proved capable of wiggling his way out of anything.

But what about Henry? Justice for him meant peace for Zach. She opened her eyes. When had she closed them? The men stared at her with varying expressions.

"Zach, I—"

He pulled her into his arms. "We're with you, Lise." He released her and kissed her forehead.

Milt squeezed her hand and smiled. "Let's get this jerk."

She nodded at Zach's father. "Lead the way."

Henry started into the forest. She fell in line behind him, followed by Zach, then Milt, and Oliver Tobias brought up the rear.

A soft crunch of leaves arose from their group. The only sign of their presence. Quiet enough the birds didn't even stop singing. Annalise took a calming breath and focused on stepping in Henry's shadow.

For over an hour, they hiked in tense silence. Annalise scanned their surroundings constantly, and she instinctively knew the men did the same. Suddenly, the mountains opened into a green valley. A sharp bluff shot from the soil and towered over an irregular pond. Ice teased the edges of the dark water.

The team froze. Annalise took in the details of the rock house. She'd never seen anything like it. What started as a cave in the bluff had been transformed into something oddly beautiful. Someone had erected a front of the house with mortar and stone that blended with the coloring of the limestone so well it almost appeared natural.

And absolutely impenetrable.

They could unload every round they had and never make a dent.

"You have a plan here?" she whispered to Henry.

"Sure do." He motioned for the group to retreat back into the brush. Then he began to lay his idea out at their feet.

Zach's gut churned as he watched his father creep into the open. This plan stunk. The scream that rose inside him, STOP!, died in his throat. Henry was right. No other option presented itself.

Lord, I'm furious. But I don't want him dead. Protect him. Protect us all.

Zach's eyebrows knitted together. Huh. He hadn't expected that prayer to pour out of his heart.

He checked to his right, making sure Annalise remained hidden. Sure enough, she crouched behind a behemoth tulip poplar. He glanced left to find Oliver Tobias similarly positioned. Milt waited a bit farther down. Nearly all of Zach's heart held its breath in individual components in this forest spread on a dreary November day. If any one of them failed to emerge from this moment, he'd be leaving part of himself behind. Kirk's blood already stained this ground.

No one else's, Lord. Please.

Henry dashed from rock outcrop to bush to tree. Zach's gaze drifted upward, to the sentinel with the big gun. Waiting. For anything that moved.

This was the plan. For Henry to bait. To grab their attention. To draw them out.

Zach did not like it.

Not one bit.

On purpose, Henry allowed the man above to catch a glimpse. Indistinct shouting rained down on them. Men, like ants, poured from the mouth of the rock house. They stopped on the precipice and glared into the field.

A shot erupted and echoed down the valley, repeating a dozen times before it faded.

Henry had dived for cover and lay safely behind a shelving of rock. Exactly as he'd planned.

Zach's body zinged with pulsating energy. He had to wait, to hold back, until Buchanan's men became more vulnerable. Until they fully emerged.

Henry shouted, "I want to speak to Buchanan!"

Laughter sounded from the thugs. One of them responded, "And just who do you think you are?"

"Tell him his scapegoat wants a word."

Zach stifled a chuckle.

One of the ants disappeared into the gaping mouth. A few moments later, two men reappeared. Zach didn't need to use the scope on his rifle to know the second was Buchanan.

"You alone?" Buchanan's words echoed off the rock.

"Just wanna talk, Jimmy Vern."

"Throw down your weapons!"

Henry tossed his AR-15 to the ground.

"All of them!"

His sidearm joined the rifle in the grass nearby. "Okay, Buchanan. Come get me!"

Zach braced for their response. Two of the thugs descended the rock steps and approached Henry's position, their gazes surveying the field. When they neared, Henry jumped to his feet and fired the gun Milt had lent him at the closest man. Buchanan's man dropped to the ground like a sack of feed corn. The second man dove for cover, and Henry retreated behind the rock.

Step two complete.

Men filed down the steps, rushing to their fallen comrade. A dozen of them half-circled the rock and pointed their guns at Henry's location.

One spokesman shouted, "No chance now! Come out!"

Henry tossed the third gun aside and rose with his hands in the air. "That was a message about how serious—"

The bullet that sank into Henry's chest blasted Zach's eardrums. In slow motion, his father grabbed at his chest, stumbled a few feet backward, and tumbled into the freezing cold pond.

"No!" Zach charged the men, firing blindly into their now-haphazard formation.

In unison, Annalise, Oliver Tobias, and Milt rushed forward, careful shots finding their targets with precision. Men dropped one-by-one.

Zach burst off the ground and swan-dived into the pond. Bolts of ice stabbed him, struck at his chest with violent heaves of pain. He cupped his hands and pulled, hard. The dark water didn't give up its secrets easily. He scanned the silty, greenish bottom for any sign of his father.

Gunshots, cushioned by the water, pounded against his ears, along with the pressure of depth. Where was he? Zach needed a breath. Now!

He shot to the surface and sucked in air. A bullet pierced the water close to his head. He retreated to the safety of submersion and scanned again. His father's dark clothing didn't help.

There!

Zach swam closer. Blood seeped from a wound in Henry's upper left chest, swirling into the water like vapor. He hooked his dad's right armpit and heaved him to the surface.

The gunshots had ceased. The silence stunned him into a motionless stupor for a few moments.

Henry choked and sputtered out a mouthful of water, then moaned.

It goaded Zach into motion. He dragged Henry's limp form to the shore.

Annalise knelt. "Zach, let me help." She took hold of Henry's shirt at the shoulders and heaved him onto the grass.

Zach's arms shook as he extracted himself from the liquid iceberg. "Is he…"

Annalise pulled her fingers from Henry's neck. "Very weak pulse. He's so cold."

Zach took in the scene between their location and the rock house. Men's bodies lay strewn everywhere. Like a battlefield, red stained the ground. "Buchanan?"

"Still in there."

"Oliver Tobias and Milt?"

"They're okay." She pointed to the top of the staircase.

Zach's teeth began to chatter. His stiff fingers probed his dad's chest, pressing hard into the hole torn there. "Go help them."

She ripped her coat off and threw it around his shoulders. "I'm not leaving you."

Chapter Eighteen

Zach's blue lips, pale skin, chattering teeth, and fear-filled eyes ripped Annalise's heart out. She needed to get him to the truck. To warmth.

Henry too.

She couldn't help them both. Zach wouldn't let her leave Henry. No way. *What do I do, Lord?*

Gunshots and shouting fell from the rock house and tumbled across the grassy slope.

"We have to move, Zach." She sat Henry up and wrapped her arms around his torso. Exhaling, she rose to her feet and dragged him toward the cover of the trees. His boot soles dug lines into the soft earth. Zach stumbled along in their wake. She reached the woods and leaned Henry against a large trunk. "Zach, your turn."

"I… okay…" He struggled to lift Henry, but fifteen or so feet later, his teeth stopped clanking together.

Temporary solution, no doubt, since Zach's clothes practically dripped icicles. When Buchanan's lair faded from sight, she signaled for him to stop and drew a lighter from her pocket.

Henry roused when Zach plopped him next to a fallen log. A faint smile crossed his lips.

Annalise's eyes grew wide. "It was you. You helped me in the snow."

He dipped his chin once.

Zach's jaw dropped.

She squatted in front of Henry. "Thank you." She returned his smile. "Let's get you warm, okay?"

His eyes slid closed.

Annalise's heart thudded as she reached to check his wrist pulse. She met Zach's gaze. A dark wave washed over her.

"Is he—?"

She shook her head.

"You're wrong, Lise. He can't be... Maybe he's just too cold." Zach stooped to gather sticks and leaves together. "Here, give me the lighter."

She handed it to him. "Oh, Zach. I'm so sorry."

"No. He's not dead." He struck the lighter into a flame and ignited the tinder. "Not after all this—"

She tried to still his hands, but he flung her off. "Let me help."

Zach melted into a curled up, shivering bundle of sobs. He handed her the lighter with a shaking hand.

After the fire caught and gobbled the twigs, she added some broken branches she'd found nearby and slipped her coat back around Zach's shoulders. "Yes."

"What?" Zach mumbled.

"I'll marry you."

He looked up at her with wide eyes. "Our timing is horrible."

She smiled. "Yes, it is." She wrung her hands. "I love you. Seeing you go into that frigid water and not knowing if you would come up... well, it was a decisive moment. I want to spend my days and nights and all my time with you. I have since I was a little girl in a sandbox full of bullies."

"I love you too, Lise. I always have. I always will."

"I have to go get Oliver Tobias and Milt."

Zach struggled to rise.

"No. You stay with Henry's... with your father." She jogged away and then turned. "I'll be back. Get warm."

Annalise forced her mind to focus on the situation with Buchanan and not be pulled backward to the love of her life and his dead, for real this time, father. She emerged from the forest again and scanned the rock face. Movement in the corner of her eye made her duck behind a boulder. She peeked out.

Buchanan.

How did he get out? Past Oliver Tobias and Milt?

Annalise's heart lurched. There was only one way. Lava boiled in her chest. Her cheeks burned. She raised the AR-15 and pinned her aim on Buchanan. Squeezed the trigger and blew out a long, slow sigh.

In the pause between breaths, she froze.

Not your job, Annalise Raven Baker.

It was as if a physical hand struck her. She slid the safety on. The AR-15 fell to her side, the strap catching it before it thudded to the ground. *Fine, Lord. I get it.* She drew her .45 and crept closer to where Buchanan now had turned to hug the bluff and sneak away. Her heart hammered and blood swooshed in her ears.

She approached the bluff, pressed her back close to it and skirted the corner slowly. To her right, a hole gaped. A tunnel exit from the rock house?

Ahead, Buchanan walked, in no hurry, alongside the jutting cliff face, headed westward.

"Stop."

He startled and spun. His face paled. Then a sneer painted across his face. "Annalise. So good to see you."

Nausea threatened her stability. "Can't say the same thing about you." She tightened her grip on the pistol between her fingers.

He took a step closer. "Gotta say, didn't see Zach's father being alive coming. Did you?"

Annalise frowned. "You're going back to prison, Buchanan. Put your hands up."

He raised them slowly with a renewed smile. "You're very persistent, Annalise. It would seem my train has reached the end of its tracks."

"So it would seem." She reached back and retrieved a set of zip ties from the side pocket on her backpack, her eyes and aim never wavering from Buchanan's face.

"Ack, I had a good run." He shoved his hands in front of him, exposing his wrists.

"Exactly how good of a run, Buchanan? Why are you walking around a free man, while Henry's on the ground, growing colder by the second?" She motioned toward the tree line with a nod of her head.

Buchanan chuckled. "It was harder than I thought to make Henry the fall guy for all this, but once it happened, it gained steam and kinda took on a life of its own. When the feds approached me and asked me to roll on everyone, to come back to the Moonshine Mafia 'undercover,' I jumped on the opportunity. Never expected ole Henry to make an appearance." He shrugged.

"So you've been, what, feeding them names but all the while restarting your role as head of the empire?"

"Pretty much."

"Duplicitous."

"Thank you."

Annalise slipped the plastic ties around his wrists. "Cinch them tight."

He grasped the free ends, one at a time, with his teeth and pulled them taught.

Annalise stepped closer and popped them a few notches tighter.

Buchanan winced.

Annalise smiled. "Let's go." She watched him closely as he turned from her to walk toward where Zach waited.

His muscles bunched, like a lion preparing to pounce.

Annalise stepped to the side just as he swung his arms toward her head. She ducked and slammed her pistol into his right kneecap.

He wailed and collapsed to the ground.

"Nice try." She rose to her full height. "Let's. Go."

"Annalise!"

She whipped her head to gaze to the left. "Oliver Tobias! Milt!" A lump of tension dissolved. "Thank goodness."

The men approached, slightly dustier and dirtier than when they'd entered Buchanan's hideout.

"You both okay?"

Milt patted her shoulder. "Right as rain."

"What happened?" she asked.

"Two men inside," Oliver Tobias responded. "They're dead now. He," Oliver Tobias gestured toward Buchanan, "slipped out, like the coward he is. There must be a tunnel or something, eh?"

Milt nodded.

Annalise pointed behind them. "Like that?"

Oliver Tobias chuckled. "Yep."

"Good work, Annalise," Milt said.

"Come on, guys. Zach's out there freezing his tail off." She lowered her voice. "Henry's dead."

The men nodded. Not much could be said anyway.

Buchanan hobbled down the hill, with her gun pressed to his back and the men flanking her at each elbow. "Better enjoy it, Jimmy Vern. It'll be the last time you see the sky without razor wire circling you."

Epilogue

"Good morning, Mrs. Leebow."

Annalise stretched. Zach kissed her forehead, and she smiled. "Good morning, husband."

The hushed whisper of waves advancing and receding outside the walls of their bungalow punctuated the joy she felt bubble in her chest.

He hugged her tighter. "Ready to go explore Puerto Rico?"

She nuzzled his neck. "Not yet. I'm rather comfortable right here."

He chuckled, then fell silent.

For long minutes, they lay listening to the tropical song greeting their morning. Zach sighed.

"You okay?"

"Mmmhmm."

"Thinking about your dad?"

"How'd you know?" He buried his face in her hair.

"I know everything about you." She giggled. "I'm proud of you."

"For what?"

"For forgiving him."

His body stiffened. "I haven't yet, Lise."

"You will. I know you, Zachary Leebow. You love your father, and now that we know everything about his life—now that we know the truth—you will." She sighed. Henry had guaranteed that the flash drive he'd given her included every detail about Buchanan murdering Jake Zucker and a mountain of evidence about the frame-up against him. It would be enough to put Buchanan under the jail for life "You would have anyway. It just makes it easier knowing he wasn't the monster we thought."

"I love you. More than you could possibly know."

She could hear the smile in his voice. "I love you too." She rose onto her elbow. "Time to go explore."

Annalise leaped from the bed, threw on her swimsuit, and raced onto the sand just outside their door. A smile stretched across her face as she stood in the honeyed warmth of the sun. The ocean waved in the glinting light, stretching as far as her eye could wander, displaying its serene turquoise invitation.

Sara L. Foust

Dear Readers,

I hope you have enjoyed continuing Annalise and Zach's story. It has been fun to write!

Pssst... Just a quick reminder, if you haven't already, please join my newsletter. I'd love to have you! Sign up now and get my free eBook novella, *Of Walls*, delivered right to your inbox. Plus get the inside scoop on all my new releases and giveaways and receive newsletters where we can connect, get to know each other, and pray for one another. Here is the link (or click on the image below): http://eepurl.com/cfqP5H

Sara L. Foust

Would you like a FREE book? For being part of my News Friends, you can receive a free ebook copy of my women's fiction novella, Of Walls.

Acknowledgments

As always, thank you, Becky, for being my first reader. Thank you to my family—all of you—for supporting me through another rollercoaster year. I'm blessed beyond measure!

About the Author

Sara is a multi-published, award-winning author, freelance editor, owner of Silver Lining Literary Services, LLC, high school English teacher, and mother of five who writes surrounded by the beauty of East Tennessee. Sara finds inspiration in her faith, her family, and the beauty of nature. When she isn't writing, you can find her reading, camping, and spending time outdoors. To learn more about her and her work or to become a part of her email friend's group, please visit www.saralfoust.com.

www.ingramcontent.com/pod-product-compliance
Lightning Source LLC
Chambersburg PA
CBHW061233170626
46809CB00007B/2652